Flowers
by the Roadside

V.T. Dacquino

A VTD EduCon Book

Published by

VTD EduCon Books

Mahopac, NY 10541

For further information go to:

www.vtdacquino.com

ISBN:10:09904814-2-5

EAN-13:978-0-9904814-2-3

Flowers by the Roadside is a work of fiction and not intended to portray any real persons or events

In Memory of

Sean Callahan

No boy has shown more courage or greater determination to keep living, and though his life was cut short at twelve, his inspiration lives on forever.

Dedication

Dedicated to my wife June
for her dedication to our lives together; and to Jamie, Vinny,
Cadence and Christian

The author gratefully expresses his appreciation to Maduranga
Nuwan of mnsartstudio via Fiverr. com for his work on the cover.
Special thanks to my colleagues of the Mahopac Writers
Workshop for their comments and suggestions and to my other
supportive friends. In particular: Janine and Dan Callahan;
Catherine Kelly; Joe Chiudina; Yanna Guo; Sonia Lynch; Karl
Milde; Andy Campbell and Meg Rowan

Contents

Flowers by the Roadside

V.T. Dacquino

CHAPTER 1

The Catskills stand in a purple-mountain-majesty high above the deep forests in central New York State guarding everything below them in God-like fashion, observing every movement of every living thing. Wildlife passes through the thick woods cautiously avoiding predators, occasionally looking up to the mountains for reassurance to avoid being eaten or shot. And little boys, like the one I was when we arrived to live in the mountains, find comfort in knowing that they're being *watched over* until they turn fourteen, and then they know they're simply being *watched*. The wind and the rivers move in rhythm with the spirits that live there. My father calls this a symbiotic symphony.

I struggle to understand, but once outdoors, a single rustling in the bushes, or the creaking of the floor boards in the barn sends out an alarm inside of me, a raising of hairs at the back of my neck, or a long line of shivers up my backbone that alerts me to the fact that I'm not alone. If I stand perfectly still, I can see them all around me. A mist that's barely visible hovers somewhere out there in the darkness, disguising them as they watch. I run terrified and cautious back to our immense, sometimes frightening 1778 farm house where my mother and father offer words of comfort. When I tell them something is out there, they tell me not to worry. No one here would harm me. They say, "It's all part of the beauty of the mountains and their land is your land. Your ability to see them is a gift. Cherish it. Listen to what they have to say."

When I turn fifteen, I see figures more clearly. The vague shifting of the wind becomes definite shapes and I know someone is out there riding the breeze. Watching me silently. I stop bringing friends home from school because I know everything we do is being observed, judged, studied. I stay in the house, but the watchers find their way in to me. They sit quietly in the shadows or roam through the basement. Their faces appear as mist on the windows and I know I can't live here anymore.

My parents tell me I shouldn't fight them. Listen. Watch. They're my friends. They would never harm me because they need me. I fight to make my parents understand how it feels to be haunted, to wake up in a cold sweat from a bad dream. Desperately, I plead with them to take me away from here, and eventually they give in and sell the house that has become an integral part of their lives.

     We are scheduled to move into 138 Dexter Lane in the village of Starlight Lake by six pm. on December 18, four days before the winter solstice. A snow squall follows my mother and me as we race along in our Escalade SUV through the roller coaster roads of the Catskills, south over route 17, then east onto Interstate 84. Snow blows across the road in front of us like a strange mist paving our way then swirls over the windshield without landing on it. Ahead of us a sign says "Welcome to Putnam County, NY" and the snow slows, then stops.

     I glance at my watch. Five seventeen.

     "It stopped snowing," my mother says suddenly. "Maybe it won't be snowing when we get there."

     "Maybe it will be," I answer.

     My father's already at the new house waiting for us and I know there will be a fire in the main fireplace and most of the big furniture will already be arranged. We're only taking up the smaller stuff. Boxes. Clothes. Mementos. The last of our belongings.

     "If it did stop snowing there," my mother says, "your father will be out clearing the driveway and we can pull right in."

     "Or not," I answer, "and the first thing I'll have to do on

our first day there is shovel. It's no better than the mountains."

My mother gives me one of those aggravated looks. "Don't do this," she says. "One of the reasons for moving is because you didn't like the weather at the old house."

"I didn't like a lot of things at the old house," I say.

"Fine," she says. "So we moved. Your fears and our troubles are behind us now. We all have to move on."

"Fine," I say, "let's all just move on."

I sit quietly and watch her as she focuses on the road ahead. She's a strong, determined woman with high cheekbones like mine. She is a strawberry blonde with warm hazel eyes that are almost green. Her nose turns up and her freckles look like they were purposely placed there. She's just turned forty and won't allow anyone to call her middle-aged or old. My father calls her a "young soul with so much to say her life has only just begun." She's an artist and her paintings are in high demand.

My father's a writer. There isn't enough room in any house for all of the books he's read and written. Not even in the huge lake house we are about to move into. I imagine him right now selecting which books will go where. He'll probably put his favorites in the book cases on either side of the fireplace. And my mother's elaborately framed mural of the Catskills with all of the faces I'm trying to run from, will go directly over the mantel.

Shortly after we exit onto the Taconic Parkway the squalls

start again and we take another exit that leads us through the back roads to Main Street in the village, to a small gathering of stores and eateries, then to a pillared entrance with a bronze sign that announces, "The Peninsula," a half mile square community that juts out onto enormous Starlight Lake, a summer mecca for boaters. A hundred houses crowd the stretch of land, each almost touching another in some places, and arrogantly avoiding each other in others.

I nervously squirm in my seat as we follow Dexter Lane, a narrow two-way road, extending snakelike in front of us. There's no method to the madness of the architecture along the way. New brick mansions and tiny lake bungalows stand side by side, the former with large stone walls protecting private parking-lot-sized-driveways; the latter with poorly painted picket fences and no driveways at all.

Exactly a half mile down the road from the main pillars, at the very tip of the Peninsula, our new house does exactly what the real estate brochure claims, "It flaunts its size and beauty with its elegant stone entrance-way that is seconded only by the grandeur of the large bay windows and multiple French doors that face the lake and in-ground pool."

It's five fifty-nine and we're on schedule, but we're stopped. A policeman is standing directly in front of our new house blocking the road. Ahead of us we can see flashing red lights and an ambulance pulled up onto the roadside near our stone wall. People are milling around everywhere with their backs to us; sirens sound from somewhere in the distance. Something awful has happened. My stomach wrenches and I search the crowd for my father. My mother nervously points to our house mouthing to a policeman that we live there and he lets her pull into our recently shoveled driveway.

I open my door and my mother tries to stop me but I jump out anyway and stand breathless in front of the countless lighted windows, seeing the night glory of our new house for the first time. But nothing seems to be happening here. I turn to walk next door through a gathering of sobbing people where a volunteer firefighter's officiously keeping people back.

Ahead of me, less than fifteen feet, a woman is screaming and people surround her trying to calm her down. But she's far from calm. She pulls away and runs to a mound of coats and blankets shouting, "My baby! They killed my baby!"

From the blankets there are legs protruding. But they aren't a baby's legs. The legs belong to a boy, thin and in jeans; the feet are wearing Nike sneakers. I can't see his face but he looks about my age.

A man comes rushing onto the scene. He's younger than my father and crying.

"John?" he cries. "Where's Johnny? Who did this?"

"A hit-and-run driver," someone says, "No one knows who did it. I didn't see anything. He was just lying there. I called 9-1-1."

The boy's father drops to his knees in front of the mound of blankets and tries to hug the lifeless boy beneath them. The boy's mother joins him.

I turn away to avoid watching, and I see my father in a light sport jacket through the crowd. He's standing next to a teenager who is staring directly at me. The boy's expression is confusing. It is a Mona Lisa smile and a long line of shivers I know too well from my time in the mountains climbs slowly up my backbone. I've seen this boy recently in my nightmares. He's wearing blue jeans with a light hooded sweatshirt despite the falling snow, and on his feet are Nike sneakers identical to the ones on the dead boy.

CHAPTER 2

The flashing red lights have been joined by the flashing blue
lights of volunteer firemen. There are people everywhere crying
and talking at the same time. The name Johnny is repeated a
hundred times, and under their voices there's something else I
hear reminding me of the whispers in the mountains. Desperately,
I try to tune them out. Johnny is still on the ground with his
crying parents; the police and EMT's try to move them away so
they can take him. I can't watch or listen anymore. I turn to leave
and am startled by my name and a hand on my arm.

  "Peter? Are you okay?" my father asks. He's come to my
side of the ambulance and he's shivering. My mother's behind
him. "We need to go in now," he says. "It's pretty cold out here.
You don't need to see all of this. Let's get into the house."

  I look around for the boy in the Nike sneakers, but he's not
there anymore. My parents lead me away through the mourning
spectators who are straining to see what's happening. Patiently,
my father squeezes us through the growing crowd. "Excuse me,"
he says to a red-eyed woman, "we need to get into our house."

The woman looks as if she's trying to recognize him and gives up, turning her attention back to the sorrow in front of her. She moves over about six inches and my father eases past her toward the Escalade as my mother and I tail behind him. He takes a deep breath and says, "We'll get the stuff in there later. I have dinner on the stove. It should still be warm."

"You cooked?" my mother says.

He looks at her and smiles half-hardheartedly. "Yeah, right," he answers. "I drove over to pick up dinner at one of the restaurants in town. You're going to like it."

She looks at him strangely and says, "When did you go? Did you see what happened next door when you went out? Did you talk to the boy?" She stops and looks nervously at me. He looks at me too, and back at her as he struggles for words. He's hiding something and I feel sick inside.

"I'm freezing out here. Let's go in," he says.

The lights are all on and there are still some cartons scattered around. The smell of new carpeting is everywhere. There's a Charlie Brown Christmas tree in the corner of the dining room and red flickering candles wrapped in pine branches on the dining room table. Dishes are set out for the three of us. It's not our good chinaware because that's still packed away in the Escalade. Poinsettias at the center of the table have a bottle of champagne sticking out of them and three glasses. "We're celebrating tonight. You can toast to the new house with us," he tells me.

I want to tell him I don't feel like toasting or partying tonight. There's a dead kid my age lying in the street next door. Does he have any idea who he is? Does he wonder how his parents are feeling right now? Does he care about what happened to him?

No one talks and we eat as if we're all afraid someone's going to mention the boy. My father pops the bottle of champagne and pours out three glasses. He lifts his and we follow. "Here's to many good years in our new house," he says.

And before I drink to his toast, I say, "And here's to Johnny. Merry Christmas."

My mother starts to cry and I excuse myself from the table and go to my room. No one stops me.

And then I cry too. I cry for Johnny and me and for what may've happened to him tonight. And also because I know that I haven't escaped from the figures in the mountains. Inside my room, there's nothing to help me feel at home. Everything's distant and strange. There's a bed that's made up with blankets and pillows, but it's not the bed or the room I know. I'm in someone elses home, someone elses life. Something tonight has changed me forever.

My bedroom is on the first floor next to my parents' room

and there are French doors leading out to a patio. I walk over and look out across the lake behind our house. The moon sheds enough light for me to see clearly that the lake's frozen, and on its surface there's a mist. Nothing's changed. They're out there watching. I want to bolt across the yard and run onto the ice with all my might and scream at them, "What the hell do you want from me?"

A voice comes from the glass doors and I peer out startled to see who may have called. It's not very audible at first and then I hear it more clearly. It says my name. Peter.

I stand for a long while gathering the courage to move. My hand is shaking and I can barely turn the door handle. But it turns. And the door opens. I grab for my coat and run out by the covered pool toward the lake. No one is out there. A cold, quiet eeriness surrounds me. Envelopes me. Instead of running back into my room, I rush around the side of the house to the front where my movements trigger the motion-sensored lights. I'm frozen by what I see there. A line of at least ten cars is stretched from Johnny's house past ours. The emergency vehicles with flashing lights and most of the crowd are gone but dozens of bouquets of flowers and candles have been placed by the roadside.

I stand motionless trying to build enough courage to walk to where the shrine's been erected. But I can't. I turn and run in the opposite direction past the waiting cars then sprint the half mile to the end of Dexter Lane stopping at the pillars that stand like the gates of heaven separating the Peninsula from the rest of the world.

Across the street there's a pizza parlor with neon lights screaming out into the night; through a large plate glass window I can see a man on the far wall behind the counter twirling pizza dough in the air. Several customers are gathered together at one table talking to a girl sitting in the center of them. She's crying. I stand there watching from across the street until I get the courage to cross and look at them more clearly. Four teenagers about my age. Three boys and a girl all with long brown hair like mine. When I reach the front of the window, one of the long-haired boys looks up at me. Nervously, I rush past the window and down the street feeling his eyes on the back of my neck.

There's a bank with a drive-in window and a sign giving the temperature and the time. It's eight twenty-six and nine degrees. Most of the shops are decorated for Christmas and closed but there's music and lights coming from a bar called "Tiny's Tavern" on the corner. The windows are high and dark and I'm unable to see inside, but I can hear loud voices singing Christmas carols off key.

My hands are suddenly cold and I dig them deeper into my coat pockets noticing for the first time since I left the house that

I'm freezing. I cross the street quickly, almost getting hit by an oncoming car with one headlight. It slows down after passing me and turns into the pizzeria parking lot. Two people get out slowly looking in my direction. Two more teenagers, a boy and a girl. I hold my breath and watch them as they join the others inside.

As I reach the pillars to enter the Peninsula, my cell phone rings scaring me half to death. I fumble for the phone and answer it.

"Where are you?" my mother shouts into the phone. "I was frightened when I saw you weren't here. I thought you were in your--"

"I'm fine," I say. "I'll be home in a few minutes." I hang up and glance across the street. Two of the teenage boys are standing at the front window, watching me watch them.

When I'm finally home, most of the cars are gone and there are flowers that stretch from my house to Johnny's, and there by the tree is Johnny himself, exactly as he had appeared by the ambulance.

My mother runs out to greet me but I need to be alone and run past her into the house.

CHAPTER 3

The hours tick by with my just sitting there in the dark staring out the glass doors at the lake. My watch reads eleven twenty-six and I know my parents have probably gone to bed or, at least, to their room. Quietly, I get up and ease my bedroom door open. Voices. I strain to separate the TV noises from my parents' conversation.

"This has to stop," my mother says from behind the closed door. "We can't keep running from it."

"It's not our place," my father answers. "The choice has to be his."

"And if it's not?" my mother asks. "What then? We let him keep running and hiding?"

"It's not up to us," my father says loudly. "Did anyone force you to do it? He has to find out why he's here and what's expected of him. It's his inheritance. I should have reached out to him the way my father did to me." He pauses. "But I was afraid that if I did---"

"Shh," my mother says. "He'll hear you."

She pauses.

"I don't know if he can handle it yet. He doesn't even

know he was chosen. Did the boy say anything to you?" my mother asks.

"I tried to get him to say something to me. But he couldn't talk. He kept looking at my face trying to figure out what was happening. He didn't seem to even know he'd been hit."

I feel my stomach twisting. I want to punch the walls as I duck back into my room to my cell phone. My father's words echo inside my head, *"He didn't even seem to know he'd been hit?"* Is my father the one who hit him? Is my father a killer?

My mother's words, *"He doesn't even know he was chosen."* ring in my head. Is it me she's talking about? What have I been chosen for? *"Inheritance?"* What have I inherited?

I sit in the chair and stare out again praying that the voice doesn't return. But it does and I refuse to be frightened by it again. "What do you want from me? Why do you keep haunting me?"

"Come out to me," the voice says from beyond my doors. And I can't avoid being scared anymore. I close my eyes and press my hands against my ears as I've done a hundred times in the Catskills and count from ten thousand until I fall asleep hoping that I won't dream of Johnny.

I am unable to sleep. Slowly, I walk to my glass doors and around the house to where his shrine is. Johnny is there by the flowers and flickering candles. Waiting. He is as excited to see me as I am to see him.

I walk quickly to where he is standing and he rushes toward me smiling, grateful I've come. His finger points excitedly to something in the flowers and he is about to speak, but before I can tell where he is pointing, I look back to find he has disappeared. I struggle to find him and notice a car parked in the street. I want to run to it but its engine starts abruptly and it pulls away. I search again for Johnny He is lying by the curb. My father is kneeling next to him and Johnny is trying to say something – until his head drops--- and he is dead.

I sit up in my bed out of breath and am startled by the light coming in from the window.

It is seven am.

My parents are still asleep. Quickly, I wash my face and brush my teeth, slip my coat on, and go out and around the house to the front. The shrine has grown even bigger; in front of it is a TV 2 News truck. A woman is talking into a small microphone and a cameraman is struggling to catch it all. When the woman sees me, she stops talking and runs over with the cameraman following close behind her.

"Excuse me," she says. "Did you know the boy who was hit here last night? I understand he was a remarkable young man. Would you be willing to say a few words about him?"

The cameraman is poised behind her and the microphone is almost touching my lips.

My mind is whirling and I can hear myself telling her that it was my father who may have hit and killed him, but I can't do it. "No," I say. "I didn't know him." And walk away leaving her standing there speechless.

When I get to the pillars and step across the street it's seven thirty-three and it's like I'm in a totally different place from the night before. The pizzeria is closed and a couple of doors down to the left of it, opposite to the corner with the bar is a diner that smells of bacon, toast and eggs. I'm almost tempted to go in but I'm stopped by a newspaper vending machine and a headline story staring back at me with a photo of a boy's face that I now know too well.

I search my pockets for seventy-five cents to buy a copy of the paper. My hands are shaking as I read:

Tragic Hit and Run Accident Stuns Peninsula Residents

At approximately 4 pm yesterday a still unidentified driver apparently struck sixteen year old Johnny Cannon, a popular Starlight Lake High School junior, causing head injuries that proved to be fatal. Reports state the boy was pronounced dead at the scene. Police have conducted a search and will be

questioning area residents in a door-to-door investigation
throughout the day today.

Reaction to Cannon's death was instantaneous. In less
than two hours after the incident, a shrine was erected by the
roadside with hundreds of flowers and candles memorializing the
popular youth. Residents of all ages prayed and wept in front of
the boy's house where the incident occurred.

A young man, identified as Luke Harper, a self-proclaimed
best friend of the boy, stated, "Johnny wasn't like anybody you
could ever know. He loved everyone and hated any kind of
violence. He was like some kind of a guardian angel to everyone
who knew him. This should never have happened to him. He was
planning a candlelight vigil on Christmas Eve and now it's going
to be a vigil for him. We're going to find out who did this. None of
us will rest until we do."

I stop reading, tuck the paper under my arm and head for
home. A couple of houses before ours, I see a police car by the
curb and two officers on a stoop talking to a woman. I hurry away
hoping they won't come to our house, but in less than ten minutes
after entering through my bedroom door, the front bell is ringing.
I check my watch. It's eight thirty-five.

"I'll get it," my mother says. She comes to my door and
knocks. "Are you awake?"

I don't answer and she goes to the front door to see who's there.

I open my door a crack to listen.

"Good morning," a deep voice says. "We're sorry to disturb you this early but we're questioning residents of the area who might know something about the accident that occurred last night. May we come in?"

"Of course," my mother says.

Chapter 4

I watch them enter the living room. The policemen, one tall and stocky, the other short and thin, have their hats in their hands and look around the house as if searching for something.

"I hope you don't mind our asking a few questions. I understand you're new here? Welcome to the neighborhood," the short one says. He offers his hand to my mother and she shakes it. "My name is officer Spencer and this is officer Cole."

"I'm pleased to meet you," my mother says. "I'm Katie Lynch."

"Mrs. Lynch, I'm sure you're aware of the terrible accident that occurred next door involving a young teenager. As you may also be aware, the person who did this is still at large and we're hoping to get some help with the investigation from anyone who might have seen or heard anything."

"I understand," my mother says. "What a horrible thing to have happened. Unfortunately, there is little we can say to help you. My son and I arrived shortly after it occurred."

"And is your son at home? We'd also like to speak with him if we may."

"Of course," my mother says. "One moment and I'll see if he's awake."

I pull the door tight and she calls, "Peter? Are you awake? Can you come out here?"

I open my door and look her straight in the eyes before I go to them. They look me over carefully. When the tall one reaches out I reach back and shake his hand. The short one has put his hat on a table and takes out a pad and pen. He writes something quickly.

"Good morning. Welcome to Starlight. I understand you arrived yesterday?" the tall one says.

"Yes," I answer.

"A boy about your age was hit by a car yesterday apparently just before you arrived here. Your neighbor, actually. Can either of you tell me what was happening when you got here? Is there anything you may have seen or overheard that might be of interest?"

My mouth is frozen and I stare at him speechless.

"It's been quite devastating for him," my mother says, "everything was just so unexpected."

"I understand," the officer replies. "It's not anything anyone wants to experience, let alone on your first day here. But, we do have to get to the bottom of this."

"Of course," my mother says. She fills him in on everything we saw and the tall one asks the big question. "Is there a *Mr.* Lynch? Did he arrive with you?"

My father suddenly appears from the kitchen and says, "David Lynch."

The tall one gives him the look he's used to.

"The writer?" he asks.

"Yes," he answers.

"My wife and I have read your books. I recognize you now from the photo on the back cover. We just bought your new one this week, *Catskill Summer,* he says. "Pretty cool stuff."

"I'm flattered," my father answers. "Perhaps I can sign it for you some time."

"That would be wonderful," he says.

"To answer your earlier question," my father continues, "I actually came here a couple of days before them to get things settled."

"So you were here when the incident occurred?" the tall one asks. The short one is writing even faster.

My father is fidgeting now and trying too hard to be calm. "Yes, well no, actually. I went out about four thirty to shovel the driveway and pick up some food for dinner because I knew my wife and son would be arriving soon. When I returned I saw

27

several people standing in the road. A man in a heavy parka was on the phone talking with someone when I walked over there. A little while later the ambulance and several police cars arrived."

I stand staring at him. *"Then when did you talk to the boy?"* I want to ask. My stomach is rumbling so loudly inside of me, I'm afraid they will hear it.

The tall one looks at the short one to be sure he's writing all of this down.

"You said you left the house at four thirty?"

"About then," he says. "The restaurant said the food would be ready by then."

"What restaurant did you say that was?" he asks.

"I believe it's called Tiny's," my father answers, "It's right in the village by the bank on the corner."

My mother suddenly interrupts and offers them coffee.

"Thank you, no," the tall one says. "Mr. Lynch did you see anything unusual when you left the house to go to the restaurant? Did you pass the house where the incident occurred?"

"No," he says. I look into his face to see if he is obviously lying.

"I left the street the same way I entered. Opposite to where the accident occurred."

"So you didn't pass the Cannon residence?"

"No," he answers.

"Did you notice if anyone was coming from the other direction?"

I wait nervously for his answer. If he is not telling the truth someone will testify against him.

My father thinks for a moment and says, "It was just getting dark and I did notice a car with one headlight coming in my direction. I had to pull over out of his way because of the narrow streets."

My stomach pulls tightly as I remember the car with one headlight in front of the pizzeria last night.

"Did you notice the make and model of the car?" the policeman asks.

"Truthfully," he says. "I really wasn't paying much attention to it. I was more concerned with getting out of his way. He was moving along at a pretty good clip and there was some light snow on the road."

The tall policeman looks at the short one again and waits for him to stop writing. "And when you got back from the restaurant, what time was that?"

"I guess about five thirty. I wasn't at the restaurant very long, but I did have a beer while the food was being wrapped."

"Did you have anything to drink before you left home? Alcohol?"

"No," my father says, "I'm not much of a drinker. I only

ordered a beer at the bar because it seemed to be what everyone was drinking there."

The tall one looks at the short one again and then at my father. "And then you came back to your house from the same direction you left?"

"I did," my father says. "I pulled into my driveway and went next door where there seemed to be some sort of commotion going on. As I said before, I walked over and a man with a parka was talking on the phone. Another man was bent over the boy who didn't seem to be moving. Minutes later, an ambulance pulled up the street and other people started arriving. A little while later my son and wife arrived."

"And you didn't notice anyone or anything that may have appeared unusual to you?"

"To be honest with you, officer," he says, "it was all unusual."

"I hear what you're saying," the officer says. "Mr. Lynch, you realize that because of the timing of your leaving the house to go to the restaurant and the time of the accident, everything you say is crucial information. We'll have to verify what you've told us against what others have seen and heard. It's likely we may have to take more time to go over all the details with you after we've talked with more of your neighbors. Would you object to coming down to the station a little later to help us put some of the pieces together? Your cooperation would be greatly appreciated."

My father's struggling again to act calm. "Certainly. I'd be happy to help in any way I can, but I'm afraid I don't know where anything is just yet. The station?"

"Maybe we can step out into the driveway. It'll be easier to explain from there."

When we are all outside, the tall policeman asks my father what car he was driving and then walks to the front of my father's Mercedes. I hurry along to join them.

Both men examine the front and then back of my father's car carefully trying to be very nonchalant about it; the short one writes something on his pad and walks to the end of our driveway to look around. Our driveway is on the right side of our house and Johnny's house is on the left. "So you say you went this way down Dexter when you left for the restaurant? Did you back out or drive out?"

"I drove out," my father says. "There were no other cars in the driveway yet and I had plenty of room to turn around."

"And you didn't notice anything unusual when you looked toward the house next door?" he gave a quick smile, "You did look both ways before crossing, right?"

"I did," my father says returning the quick smile, "but it was already getting dark and I didn't really see anyone out there or anything unusual."

Both policemen stand there for a few moments and the tall one asks the short one if he got everything. Finally, the tall one asks my father again if he wouldn't mind coming down to the station at about four pm to help them piece together all of their facts.

"That would be fine," my father says.

The tall one gives my father quick directions before shaking his hand and mine. "I'm going to hold you to that autograph, Mr. Lynch. And welcome again to the neighborhood."

My father puts his hand on my shoulder and the three of us watch as they drive off toward Johnny's house.

Chapter 5

When we get back into the house my father wipes his brow and loosens his collar.

"Did you do it?" I ask him. "Did you hit him and leave the scene?"

He looks at me as if I've punched him in the stomach.

"What?" he says. "Do you think I could kill that boy and just drive off?"

"Your father would never do that. How could you even think he could?" my mother asks.

"I heard you," I say. "I heard you say you tried to speak to him and he couldn't answer you. You had to have been there when he was hit. I'm not stupid!"

I fight my urge to cry and feel myself shaking; when he comes to hug me I push him away. My mother is crying now and I have never been more scared or confused. I feel as if I'm in one of my wild dreams praying that I will wake up.

"I just want you to tell me the truth. I don't want you to lie to me."

My father takes my arm and leads me to the couch. "I would never lie to you, Peter. But there is something we need to talk to you about. We should have had this talk a long time ago but – I – we – your mother and I were trying to protect you."

"From being the chosen one? From my inheritance?" I ask.

They are both stunned.

"I heard you talking last night," I say.

He is running his fingers though his hair and looking to my mother for help.

"We didn't know if it was our place to tell you." He stops and looks again at my mother before starting again. "Maybe we should have just been honest. We aren't like other people. Your mother and I have special abilities." He pauses. "And so do you. We just didn't know when you would realize what you were. When you would arrive at your awakening."

"What are you talking about?" I shout. "I don't know what the hell you're even talking about." My head is pounding and I feel as if I'm going to puke. Nothing is making sense and I want to run out of there away from them; when I try to stand, my father turns me gently to face him.

"I did try to speak to Johnny last night at the accident, but he was already dead. Your mother and I have been able to communicate with the dead since before we were your age. It just seemed to happen naturally for us. We never experienced the resistance you've experienced."

"Your father and I both started seeing and communicating with the dead when we were fourteen and it just came naturally to us. I don't know why it is taking you so long. Why you are so afraid of your gift."

"Gift?" I said. "Gift? Do you call communicating with dead people a gift?"

"Peter," my father said. "Your name wasn't chosen by us at random. I named you after my father who also had our gift. You were chosen for an assignment and you need to accomplish it. It will likely be the first of many missions you'll accomplish. Many lost souls have been waiting for your arrival."

"I still don't know what you're trying to say," I shout. My heart is pounding and nothing they are saying makes sense to me.

"I have something for you to read," my father says. "I know you don't like reading my books but this is a set of emails I wrote when I was about your age. Because of my father's sudden death I felt I had to reach out to someone to talk to. I chose a paranormal I found on line and asked him in a series of emails all of the questions haunting me. I think you should read them. They'll answer a lot of important questions for you about me,

35

your grandfather, our special gift, how your mother and I met, and most importantly what we believe is our purpose in life. They're all in order from about the time my father died and read something like a diary. I've since organized them into what I call Diary Poems but I think for now you should start with the emails themselves. The emails and the Diary Poems were all meant just for you so that you could someday understand our past and what it was like for me growing up. I'm sorry I didn't give them to you sooner," he says.

It's nine thirty-seven and I ask to be left alone in my room. But I am alone for less than five minutes when my father raps softly on my door.

"I want to be alone, I say. "I understand," he says. "I just want to give these to you." I open my door and he hands me a manilla envelope. I reach inside and pull out printed pages of emails. The first page says:

EMAILS TO A PARANORMAL written by Damien Darrk

I look up at him and he reads my confusion.

"It's a pseudonym," he says. "I didn't want to use my real name to write the emails since they were written to a paranormal I didn't actually know. You'll understand when you read them." He smiles sadly. "I realize if you read these it will the first of any of my written works you've actually read, but I promise these are very different from the rest of my work and will hold your interest. They are about important details in my life when I was about your age and it all directly relates to you. I believe this will tell you things you have the right to know. I eventually wrote them out, like I said, in ten line poems with ten poems to a section and three sections to a chapter called Diary Poems. I can give them to you to read at another time, but these are the actual emails. You don't have to read them if you choose not to, but I wish you would. For your sake and ours. Don't hesitate to ask us questions."

He pulls the door closed and I stand there like some kind of statue staring at the pages of emails.

At nine forty-seven I sit nervously at the edge of my bed and begin reading.

TO: Paranormalinsite2@email.com
FROM: DamienDarrk@info.org

I know you may find my name to be strange and may think that no caring parent would name a child Damien Dark. The fact is, I've created this name to protect my identity and will tell you my real name only when I know you can be trusted.

I've chosen you to receive these emails because of your reputation as an author and lecturer. I believe as you do that there are no coincidences when it comes to matters of the supernatural. I also believe that dead people live here.

I have been visited by a spirit who is trying to

communicate with me. I believe she is a young girl in desperate need of connecting. The reason she has chosen my room and me, a seventeen year old boy, is why I am coming to you.

She'll come again tonight after midnight when the house is quiet, whispering behind my closet door, and moaning too as she's done for months. I'm not afraid and know I have to help her but I am helpless without you.

I stop reading to look quickly at my closet door. Did my father actually see ghosts in his closet? Is my "inheritance" an ability to see and hear ghosts? Why wouldn't he have said something to me earlier? I continue reading.

She came to me several months ago on Oct 30, the night of my birthday. My mother threw a surprise party with my closest friends, all geeks. When it was over I went to my room where something called to me from my closet, moaning.

I wasn't sure what I was hearing. And then I laughed to myself thinking I was being pranked.

"Come out," I said. "I know you geeks are in there."

But no one answered, and the moaning continued.

I pulled the covers off and walked to the door at the foot of my bed. The moaning got louder.

I felt a coldness coming from the closet, but not like any coldness I've ever felt. It seeped through my skin and entered me from every pore. I reached for the doorknob wishing to end the silly prank, but the knob was already turning and the door opened to an almost empty room.

My clothes hung from hangers like ghosts, unmoving. The shelf above them was motionless, and from somewhere on the floor in the corner of the darkness the moaning became a whimper, like a puppy without his mother, crying for help.

I dropped to my knees and listened as the whining took on a strange rhythm, song-like, childlike, a lullaby that mothers use to quiet their children. And then there was silence. Until I heard my own mother's voice behind me.

I gave her a poor excuse for kneeling by my closet at midnight and have given her a dozen more excuses for my strange behaviors. She doesn't understand any of this so I'm turning to you to shed some light on the mystery that is haunting my room–and me.

Chills begin at the base of my spine and crawl up so

quickly I think they will burst through the top of my skull. Did my father really write this? Did he really see ghosts? Are these emails for real? Memories of the figures in the Catskills come rushing into my head and I feel myself shaking. Is this what will be next for me? Is my father telling me that ghosts will start appearing in my closet the way this girl appeared to him? Why did she come to him? He said his mother didn't understand him. That could only mean that my grandmother didn't "inherit" the "gift."

When I lift my head, I am knocked breathless. Johnny is staring at me with his Mona Lisa smile through my glass doors. I should be screaming in fear, but there is an eerie calm running through me as I stand staring back at him--- until a knock at my door breaks the silence--- and Johnny disappears. I run to the doors but no one is out there.

Chapter 6

It is ten twenty and my father enters my room. I stare at him.

"You saw them too," I say.

"Most of my life," he answers.

"Why didn't you tell me?" I ask him.

He turns his head unable to look at me and says, "It's in the emails. My father had the "gift" when he was young too. When I turned fourteen things began to appear as they did for you. I told my father and he started to teach me how to deal with them. He called them "tortured souls" who needed us. He was there to answer many of my questions the way I should have been there for you, but after he died I was left on my own and had to turn to a paranormal to find answers to my own questions."

He stops talking and takes a step toward me but I step back from him. He continues talking. "When I was seventeen my father was hit and killed in his car in an accident on his way home from a business trip. It was the night of my birthday. I miss him until this day." He stops talking and then continues again. "I know your mother says I shouldn't, but I blame myself for his death. I think that maybe if he didn't tell me all he did – if he didn't help me to be an Earth-Bound Angel---"

I look up at him quickly.

"That's what we're called," he says. "Your mother's one, too."

She suddenly appears in the doorway.

"I'm sorry we didn't tell you all of this sooner," she says. "Your father was worried that if he told you he would have served his purpose on earth the way his father did and be taken from you."

"So you let me go on being afraid?" I ask.

"We didn't expect you to be as afraid as you were. Neither of us had that experience," my mother says. "We may have been frightened at first, but we eventually understood our mission and we were made to understand and accept who we were. Please believe us when we say the spirits are not here to harm you. They need you. I suspect now that the delay in your acceptance of them, and our moving to this house, was part of a larger plan that has something to do with Johnny's death."

"Will I continue to see them? Will they start appearing in my closet the way that girl came to Daddy or come to my back door the way that Johnny came to me?"

They both look surprised. "He came to you while you were awake?" my father asks.

"Just before you knocked," I say.

"Did he speak to you?"

"Not then," I answer. "but he has spoken to me. He said my name. Why?"

"Spirits usually come to your father and me through our dreams, especially when we were younger, but things may be different for you."

Anger begins to rise inside of me and I lose my patience for all of this. "Why the hell is this happening to me? Why couldn't you tell me all of this before? What kind of freaks are we?"

My mother rushes to me and I let her hug me.

"We're not freaks," my mother says. "We're angels on earth sent to do missions, to help spirits cross-over, and you--- you Peter—have the potential to be one of the most important missionaries of all since you are a pure Earth-Bound Angel, born to two Earth-Bound Angel parents."

I ask them to please leave me alone now and they go away quietly. As soon as they do, I sit and try to make sense of everything I've learned. But it's useless. I return to the emails and read more of them to learn the details of my grandfather's death. My memory slips to the photo of him on the fireplace mantel in

43

our Catskill home. His eyes in the photo are so real, so piercing, I could never bear to look into them. "When did he die?" I asked once, "and how?"

"He died in a car accident my mother said, but Daddy doesn't mention it because it hurts him to talk about it."

I never asked him or her about my grandfather again.

I feel something inside of me begging me to go to my grandfather's photo, to stare into his eyes for answers, but the photo is packed somewhere in the moving cartons; I make a mental note to find it later, and then skim to the part where my father has asked to see his father's body.

TO: *Paranormalinsite2@email.com*
FROM: *DamienDarrk@info.org*

The police said my mother had to go to the morgue to identify the body, and I made her take me to see if I could reach him. He was on a table with a sheet over his face, and when they lifted it we saw him.

He did not appear to be asleep. His eyes were closed and his face was badly bruised, no frown or anger, or smile, an expressionless face, like the girl in my closet.

I tried to make him hear me, quietly, from inside my head. And waited for his answer, but it didn't come.

And I screamed silently,"Are you okay?" But there still was no answer and I stood there waiting until I was led away crying.

And then I'm crying too. I want to tell him it's okay, but I know it isn't. I try to imagine what it would be to suddenly lose my father. I want to run into the next room to tell him how grateful I am to still have him. For the first time in my life, I realize I could lose him at any second and wonder if he would be able to communicate with me after his death.

I try to absorb what I've read. My parents saw ghosts too. They know that everything I said about the spirits in the woods is true. The spirits are there and they have watched everything I've done since I was born. And then I remember the girl in my father's closet. Was the girl in the closet connected to my grandfather? Was she put in the closet by him to communicate with my father? Why didn't my grandfather personally communicate with my father if they both had the "gift." Why did my father have to turn to an outsider for help?

I thumb through the pages and hope that somewhere in this manuscript there are answers; I need to know if my grandfather finally contacted him, but I'm stopped by the scene at the funeral parlor, and my father's questions and comments to the paranormal.

I don't know what religion you are. We are Catholics. When people we love die, we take them to be embalmed and put them in their caskets with the lid open for people to see. Friends and relatives came for two days to see my father's body surrounded with beautiful flowers from everyone. They stood in line to get the chance to kneel and see his face close up one last time before never seeing him again.

The room was filled with chairs and I sat in the front row with my mother to hug and kiss and shake hands with all of the guests who came to pay their respects. Between the hugs I sat and stared at him waiting.

On the morning of his burial, I didn't want to go to his grave site. I had never been to a cemetery. My father didn't like going there. He told me I wasn't ready for it either. And when his hearse pulled in, our limousine followed and I knew why I should have listened.

My mind is spinning with words I want to say to my

father. I think of him looking at the body, crying. I've never seen my father cry. Sadness builds in me and I want to call out and tell him to come into my room so I can tell him I'm sorry about what happened to his father and even sorrier that we are not as close as they were. I want to say I love him and would do everything I could to contact him if anything were to happen. The way he did for his father. But I sit there silently thinking until a new thought rushes into me. Will Johnny's parents have a wake and funeral for him? Will people expect our family to attend since we are now his neighbors? Will I have to go to a funeral parlor to see Johnny's body? What if he tries to talk to me there? I try to push the thoughts away by returning to the letters. But my father's emails about his trip to the cemetery are even more disturbing than his last email.

Their voices began in chaos at the gate, all of the spirits talking at once, a cacophony of frantic questions from everywhere, hundreds of voices penetrating my skull. I pressed my hands against my ears trying to block them out but the voices came from somewhere deep inside my head.

I couldn't bear to hear them and screamed for them to "STOP!" And the driver did. I ran from the car back to the gate with my mother shouting behind me.

She let me run. I stood outside the cemetery gasping for air until the voices were finally silent.

I stare at my door. Was it true? Could he hear the voices of the dead in a cemetery? Have I inherited that too? I have never been in a cemetery. Will dead souls scream out to me to help them if I go there? Will I have to finally go to the cemetery if I attend Johnny's funeral?

Before I can even attempt to answer my own questions, the front doorbell rings. I remain quiet and nervously listen to see who is at our door. Soon I hear footsteps coming to my room. My mother raps softly. "Peter? There are some people here to see you. Teenagers."

I grab a long-sleeve black sweater from my closet and slip it on.

Chapter 7

It is eleven twenty-five when I reach the front door. Four teenagers, one girl and three boys, are standing there staring at me. Each is wearing black and each has long, straight hair the color of mine nearly touching his or her shoulders. The girl is amazing. Her hazel eyes are haunting and strangely familiar as she meticulously scrutinizes me from head to toe; she looks like something out of a 1970's rock group from my father's old record albums.

"My name is Maggie," the girl says. "You must be Peter."

"I am," I say.

She points to the tallest of the boys on her right. "This is Luke."

He reaches out his hand for me to shake and I do. We are about the same height. He has a strong grip and I grip him back to show him I am not a wimp. He smiles and I suddenly remember his name from the newspaper article about Johnny's death. He is

Johnny's, "self-proclaimed best friend."

"And this is Mark and Paul," she says. They also reach out to shake my hand, but they don't squeeze.

"Officers Cole and Spencer told us they were here to see you earlier. Did they tell you about the candlelight vigil for Johnny?" Maggie asks.

"I read it in the paper," I say.

"Johnny was our best friend. He was one of us," she says. "We're asking everyone to light a candle in his honor on Christmas Eve. Will you do it?"

"Of course," I say. "Do you need me to do anything else?"

She turns away from me to look at the other three. They nod a hesitant yes to her and she says, "We're meeting at the pizza parlor at six tonight to discuss it. We know you know where it is. We saw you there last night. Can you come?"

"Sure," I say.

They all nod "yes" again and turn to leave. I watch as they walk toward the road. After they walk off, I turn to go back in the house. My mother is smiling and waiting for me to say something.

"They seem very nice," she says.

"They seem very strange," I answer. "I'm going to meet with them at the pizza parlor at six."

"That's good," she says. "You should make friends here."

She pauses. "I think your father wanted you to go to the police station with him at four, but I know he'll understand. Do you need money for food?"

"I'm fine," I say, and before I escape to my room, she adds, "Do you want to talk about—about the things we told you?"

"No," I answer. "you should have talked to me about that a long time ago when I came to you up in the mountains to tell you I was scared."

She's speechless and I leave for my room then slam the door behind me.

My anger rises then dissipates as I sit on my bed. Who *is* she? Who am *I*? How could I have lived all of these years without even knowing who or what I was, and who or what my parents are?

It is eleven fifty-five. I have over six hours before meeting with Maggie and the boys; I pick up the emails to try to find some answers. I turn to a page about my grandfather, but I can't bear to read anymore about my grandfather's death. My head is spinning with the details I have already read about him. I fumble through the pages and stop at a page about my father's getting *fixed up* for the senior ball by my grandmother!

TO: Paranormalinsite2@email.com
FROM: DamienDarrk@info.org

My mother's friend's cousin wants to meet me. My mother said she will be the perfect date for the Senior Ball. She has a really great personality, which in mother-talk means she is probably the ugliest girl in her graduating class.

I hear myself laughing out loud and it helps to relieve tension. I am eager to read what my grandmother's blind date for my father looked like.

I wanted to tell her that I had changed my mind. I didn't want to go to the stupid Senior Ball but she said I should get out of the house. I would really like her. She is fun to be with and has blonde hair and piercing eyes.

When the doorbell rang, my heart nearly stopped. I knew who was on the doorstep. My mother had invited her friend's cousin's daughter Katie to dinner so we could get to know each other before our first date.

The girl's name is Katie? – my mother's name! Did my grandmother fix my father up with my mother on a blind date? Why didn't I ever know this?

I felt the sweat beading up in my arm pits and my

hand was actually shaking when I opened the door. I must tell you that I half suspected that I would see the ghost girl from my closet pretending to be Katie. But there they were, mother and daughter, neither of them even coming close to looking like my ghost girl.

I guess I was staring because my mother said, "Where are your manners? Invite them in."

Katie wasn't anything I imagined. I wanted to take a picture of her and send it to the geeks. They would have crapped their pants and said I rented her for the photo. Then reality hit me. Did you ever realize you were too awake? Did you wish you really were dreaming because what you were experiencing was too good to be real? Why would someone like Katie ever want someone like me? And then I glimpsed her in the mirror behind me. She was shaking her head "yes" at her mother.

My ghost has long blonde hair and piercing blue eyes. Katie is a strawberry blonde with warm hazel eyes that are almost green. Her nose turns up and her freckles look like they were purposely placed there. Do you believe in love at first sight?

I couldn't take my eyes off of her and my mother gave me the "Don't-Do-That" look. But I did it anyway and I think Katie liked it because she was staring back at me. Both her eyes and her freckles looked like they were *dancing.*

I feel myself smiling big-time trying to picture my parents as teenagers staring at each other. And then it hit me. Maggie, the girl on the doorstep, has my mother's hazel eyes.

After dinner our mothers let us take a walk together and I can't believe I took her hand as we walked – and she let me. "I didn't think you would be so good looking," she said. I was so surprised I squeezed and almost broke her hand.

"I never even came close to thinking you were as good looking as you are," I said. But she wasn't listening; she was making a face and holding her hand.

I'm smiling again and I feel I'm being taken to a time I should have known about. Why did I never let them share their important moments with me?

I told her I was sorry and then I said, "Squeeze mine." And she said, "What?"

I said, "I want to be sure I'm not dreaming. Squeeze my hand." She smiled an amazing smile and I said, "Will you come to the dance with me?"

And now I'm trying to make a mental note to tease my father about this, too. "Squeeze my hand so I know I am not dreaming!" I can't even picture my father saying something like that – and my mother liking it!

When we got back into the house, my mother asked if we enjoyed our walk. "It was okay," I said, and Katie looked shocked, so I burst out laughing and she smacked me. She actually smacked me, and we both cracked up laughing. When she left to go home I wished she didn't.

I told my mother I really liked Katie and hurried to my room because I knew something was not right. It was too perfect. Too unreal. No noise was coming from the closet so I sat on my bed and expected the ghost girl to appear and the dream to suddenly end.

I'm happy to be learning about how they met, but I'm sad too because I realize how little I know about them. I want to go to them and say I'm sorry for not talking to them about my own life when they asked, and for not wanting to see picture albums of all of us when I was little or hear about their happy times. Did I ever ask my mother about her paintings or read my father's books? I pushed my parents away from me. I take up the emails and try to learn more about them – and me.

Chapter 8

It is one thirty pm. As I search for a place to start reading, my father's voice comes through my doorway.

"Peter? Can I come in?"

"Yes," I say.

"He walks over and sits on the bed then looks at the pages in my hands. "Hows the reading going?" he asks.

"All right," I answer.

"Any questions? Did you find out anything you didn't know?"

I want to say yes. I try to think of all the questions I was going to ask him. There's something I want to tease him about, but I can't remember what it was.

"Your mother said some local teenagers came to see you and you're going to meet with them. That's good. I was going to invite you to come with me to the police station but meeting with them is more important," he says.

"Did your father ever contact you?" I hear myself ask. "Who was the girl in the closet?

He gives me a half smile because he now knows I've been reading his emails.

"It's all a long story," he says. "There's a lot more for you to read. I prayed if I had a son of my own someday he would never have to go through what I went through. I was devastated when my father died, especially since we had finally connected. You can imagine how I must have felt when I couldn't contact him."

"Why wouldn't he answer you?" I ask.

"I didn't know what that was all about until a long time later. Hopefully, you'll read about it soon." He pauses. "I think it would make more sense for you to read it than have me try to explain it to you."

I don't agree, but I am not ready to argue with him.

"I thought the way you met Mom was pretty funny in some places," I say.

He smiles.

"And what does the girl in the closet mean? Will I be seeing ghosts?"

"You already have," he answers. "I suspect that Johnny is to you what the girl in my closet was to me. She was my first assignment. I hope you'll be reading how her story unfolded for me and how my role became clearer through my dreams of her."

"Will Johnny be explaining my mission through dreams?

Is he *my* mission?"

"I suspect dreams may play a role, but to be honest I don't know exactly how it will work for you. I'm sure, though, you'll find out soon enough. Have you read much about the girl in my closet, yet?"

"Some," I say. "I've been jumping around. I've read about your father, how he died and how you tried to contact him, and how you and Mom met. I also read something about the girl coming into your dreams."

"Read more about the girl," he says. "It will give you an idea about how my first mission went and what you may expect yours to be."

"Why do you keep saying mission?" I ask.

"Some people die with their connections to this life still unsettled. Until they get their issues resolved they're stuck in a sort of limbo. They're unable to cross over to the next life."

"And Earth-Bound Angels help them to cross over?"

"Yes," he says. "It's our mission, like I said to you. You don't have to help them if you don't want to. Your mother and I never questioned it. We just sort of accepted it." He looks into my eyes and asks, "How are you dealing with all of this? Are you still afraid? Is it something you'd rather not do?"

"I have no idea," I say. "this all sounds kind of crazy to me."

"I understand," he says."No one will force you to do anything."

I see his disappointment and I can't hurt him. "Would you help me if I tried to help them?" I ask.

He looks surprised and pleased. "There's nothing in this world your mother and I would want more. We can probably answer any questions you might have."

He tries not to show his excitement and I know he wants to hug me, but it's too weird at my age and I can't do it. "I'm a little worried about Johnny's funeral," I say. "Will I have to go to a funeral parlor and cemetery for him? Will he or other spirits try to talk to me from their graves?"

"I won't lie to you," he says. "It could happen. I was pretty freaked out the first time it happened to me. I covered my ears and tried to block them out but I couldn't. I avoid going to cemeteries whenever I can. It's just that they know you might be able to help them, even though it doesn't really work that way. Most missions are assigned. Spirits select you from other Earth-Bounds. My girl selected me and so have many others. I imagine Johnny has chosen you."

"Oh, great," I say.

"You don't have to do anything you don't think you can handle. If it's too challenging for you, don't do it."

I look into his eyes and say, "It depends on what I have to

do. I don't even know what any of this is about. Maybe I shouldn't be getting involved with dead people." He looks disappointed so I say, "I have to see what happens. I guess if you and Mom can handle it, I can too."

He smiles and I know he is relieved that I'll consider it.

"Don't be too happy too soon," I say. "I still don't know what the heck is going on and whether I will be able to deal with it all. What does he expect me to do for him?"

"Only Johnny can answer that. But he evidently believes you can. You're the son of two Earth-Bounds. You'll be surprised what you're capable of doing. Your mother and I have never been sorry about doing what we do. I honestly believe the only reason you haven't come out of your shell until now is because the time wasn't ripe for your mission. Everything that's happened has occurred in the order and time it had to. Including the selling of our house and Johnny's death. Don't blame yourself for any of it. All that's happened was meant to happen."

"Well, it would have been better if it were a lot less weird," I answer.

He smiles and says," Keep reading and let me know if you have any questions; let me know how things go with the neighborhood kids. Remember, nothing happens in isolation. To everything there's a purpose; there is no such thing as coincidence."

"I'm meeting them at six," I say. "I probably could go with you to the police station at four and still meet them."

"I'd rather you concentrate on meeting those kids," he says. "I don't anticipate any problems with the police. I didn't do anything wrong," he says. "I'm sure whoever did this will be caught."

"I hope so," I say.

"We'll exchange stories when we both get back from our meetings." He stops talking and looks over at me. "I'm sorry if we handled this all wrong for you," he says.

"Is there any *right* way to handle this?" I ask.

He gives me his half-smile. "I don't think so. Let's hope we can do better as this whole thing unfolds. It would be good to have you as a team member," he says.

"Do I have a choice?" I ask.

"Always," he answers.

He starts to leave the room and I stop him. "You never said whether your father actually contacted you," I say.

He gives me one of those "READ THE EMAILS" looks.

"Fine," I say. "I'll read the emails!"

He smiles a great smile and this time I give him an uncomfortable half-hug; he gives me a real hug back.

When he leaves the room I stand staring at the door. I'm relieved by the things he's said and a strange excitement runs through me. It's almost as if I'm becoming someone else. I'm not so afraid anymore; I feel ready for whatever's coming. I look to my glass doors for Johnny, half-expecting him to be there so I can tell him I'm willing to listen to what he has to say, but he doesn't appear.

I eventually pick up the pages and start reading more about my parents and grandparents, getting more and more riveted to his story. And then chills climb up my spine as he begins asking the paranormal about dead people and the girl in the closet.

TO: Paranormalinsite2@email.com
FROM: DamienDarrk@info.org

How closely do I have to listen to hear their whispers in the wind or separate the ticking of the clock from the tapping of their fingers on my brain? Or recognize that I must be dreaming when the girl from the closet floats close enough to brush my cheeks with hers?

Have you ever lost someone you loved? Do you feel them when you lie awake in the night? Do they talk to you in words or come in cold rushes through you? And do they pull across your skin like a ballerina's tights hugging closely to you making it impossible for you to breathe?

Suddenly, my own breath is taken away and I gasp for air as I take in his words. I 've never actually been touched by any of the spirits I've seen and heard. Is this what I can expect to happen next? Will Johnny pull across my skin and try to enter me like some freaking ballerina? I sit and struggle to breathe taking several deeper breaths before reading again.

TO: Paranormalinsite2@email.com
FROM: DamienDarrk@info.org

I haven't heard back from you but I know how busy you are. I check your web site to follow your activities. You'll be speaking tonight about the ghosts in your book at a local coffee house. Please make time to write to me. She knows I've contacted you. Her whining was deafening but it has quieted some, and she ventures out more often hovering around my room avoiding contact and clinging desperately to the walls like a blown up balloon rubbed against a kid's hair charged with static electricity.

She came at first as a face without an expression, floating above me and I awoke in my bed sweating and startled but not afraid of her. I knew somehow she wasn't there to harm me

I sit there in disbelief as my own recurring dreams spin in my head. Were my dreams actually spirits fighting to communicate? I try to remember the many times I jumped up in my bed, panting and fighting for air in a cold sweat. I press myself to remember specific details and a chill runs through me like ice water. There is no question that Johnny has appeared to me in my dreams before we ever left the old house. Did I see him before he actually died? Did he know what was about to happen? I strain to continue.

She has now learned how to enter my dreams. I see her as she must have looked before her death, pretty with long blonde hair hanging to her shoulders and blue piercing eyes.

She is running alone, laughing. It is a wonderful sound that echoes as if in a tunnel. A pink ribbon is in her hair and it bounces as she runs. She stops at a swing set in the woods and mounts the swing with her hands on the chains high above her head perfectly still and still perfectly expressionless. Not swinging, until a man comes up to her and makes her smile. He is a shadow at first as if the dream is taunting me into believing the stranger is my father, and then he becomes clearer. He walks behind her and begins to push her higher and higher and her laughter with his is music.

It is not my father but I am glad for her. His face and hers are filled with happiness as the swing swings even higher. Until he stops it from moving and she runs from it and him across the lawn going faster and faster. I watch him alone at the swing staring after her. Sad. His short dark hair thinning and parted on the left, his beard a shadow on a handsome face.

And then she is alone again standing by a wooden bridge, her hands on her face, and she is crying, no, whimpering. And I recognize those sounds. I sit up in my bed and listen as the whimpers come through my closet door.

Chapter 9

Messages. Communications from the world of the dead and almost dead. A sudden image of a boy's face rushes into my mind. Johnny! I want to put the manuscript down and run from the house to keep him from flooding my thoughts, but I think about the conversation with my father and become calm again. I've been chosen for a mission and held by a need to keep reading, a hostage of the questions my father and the manuscript have posed for me. I need to know the meaning of the girl in his closet and what it has to do with me. What did she want from my father? Desperately, I try to recall my latest dream of Johnny.

I am unable to sleep. Slowly, I walk to my glass doors and around the house to where his shrine is. Johnny is there waiting for me by the flowers and flickering candles. He is as excited to see me as I am to see him.

I walk quickly to where he is standing and he rushes toward me smiling, grateful I've come. His finger points to something in the flowers and he is about to speak, but the expression on his face changes to fear. I walk quickly to where he is standing; he rushes toward me smiling nervously. He points again excitedly, but before I can tell where he is pointing, I look back to find he has disappeared. I struggle to find him and notice a car parked in the center of the street. I want to run to it but its engine starts abruptly and it pulls away. I search again for Johnny. He is lying motionless in a pool of blood. My father is kneeling next to him and Johnny is trying to say something---until his head drops---and he is dead.

I sit confused forcing myself to remember every detail. To think. The dream was at the shrine. Before the car came, he was pointing. Pointing at what? Fear runs through me. Mountain-type fears. I know what I need to do but I am reluctant to do it. Slowly, I force myself to the glass doors, the street, and finally the shrine.

There is no one in front of Johnny's and the shrine sits the same way it did in my dream. I pray that he doesn't appear as I walk toward it and reach the spot where he stood with my father. I rerun the dream like an old movie. Johnny is pointing to a place near a tree and there by a large display of flowers and candles I see a framed photograph of Johnny with Maggie just as she appeared on my doorstep.

I reach for the photo, but there are voices coming from

Johnny's house; I panic and run off to the back of my house with the framed photo still in my hand.

I'm shaken and confused when I reach my room. Why was Johnny pointing to this photo with Maggie? What was he trying to say about her? Was Maggie Johnny's girlfriend?

I sit in my room thinking and thinking and nearly drive myself mad with questions. Johnny's face in the photo is haunting as I study it for clues. His lips look ready to part and say something; I turn quickly away from his face and go to Maggie's face. She's beautiful; her eyes are staring into mine nearly hypnotizing me, forcing me to keep staring. Finally, I tuck the photo under my mattress and pick up my father's emails to distract myself. Randomly, I open to a page and begin reading more about my father's resident ghost.

TO: *Paranormalinsite2@email.com*
FROM: DamienDarrk@info.org

Her name is Melinda. I don't know how I know this but it came to me in another dream. Someone was calling her Melinda and she was standing over me staring, her eyes looking into mine. She was expressionless again. Nothing betrayed her thoughts. And then slowly her lips began to move upward and her smile, beautiful and haunting, woke me.

I sat up with an urgency to call your number. I found it on your web site and memorized it for times like this. But the clock said midnight and I knew I couldn't call. I wished that you would finally answer my emails.

I trust you to know what I am experiencing. My mother's concerned and I will never get her to believe that spirits like Melinda live here. They call on people like us for help. It is perfectly natural for those of us willing to believe.

The words, "It is perfectly natural for those of us willing to believe" echo in my head. I sit quietly trying to make sense of what I am reading, trying to believe in my father's first mission – and mine.

Do you hear her? A voice that calls out from somewhere. Soft moans or whining that reaches deep inside of you begging, pleading for you to understand? A soft whisper that says Melinda. Or maybe Melinda isn't the one calling to you. Maybe you hear a male voice. A father who is calling out to his son. A desperate plea for you to talk to me.

Was my grandfather responsible for the girl in the closet?

Did he send her and the paranormal because he wasn't able to personally communicate with my father?

Billy Joel sang, "Only the Good Die Young." I play it often in my room. Have you spoken to many dead people who have died young? Are they still here to talk about their lives? Will they be okay? Did my father die because he was good?

When you were young did your parents say, "Finish everything on your plate or you will stay there until you do." Does God keep us here until we finish everything we have started?

I look up and out my glass doors. Why was my grandfather taken so young? Was he too good to be suffering? Did he complete all of his missions and get taken away as some sort of reward? Do only troubled souls contact Earth-Bound Angels for help? How old do you have to be to be an Earth-Bound Angel? I turn to the emails for an answer thumbing quickly to find the right place.

TO: Paranormalinsite2@email.com
FROM: DamienDarrk@info.org

The voices began when I was fourteen. My father

is the only one who knew I heard them. He told me not to be afraid. He said they were lost and lonely spirits and that his voices began at fourteen too.

"Does everyone hear voices?" I asked my father.

"No," he said. "You and I were chosen. We are special."

"Do you only see them in your dreams?" he asked

"Yes," I said.

"Do they scare you?"

"No," I answered.

"Good," he said. "You needn't be afraid."

Suddenly, I'm no longer afraid. I feel the connection I have with my father and my grandfather. We were all about fourteen when we first began seeing and hearing spirits, and we were all chosen to help tortured souls. I am my father's son – and my mother's, too. I thumb again quickly through the emails to see how old she was when she first knew she was an Earth-Bound Angel, ---but I stop myself. I remember she said she was fourteen. I need to stay on task and find out why Melinda came to my father's closet. And why Johnny has come to me.

"Who are they?" I asked

"People with a message," he said. "Some have come for your help. Do you want to help them?"

"Yes," I said.

"Good," he answered, "me too. We are their Earth-Bound Angels. Come to me if you have any questions. I will be here for you."

I repeat the words out loud to the quiet of my room. Earth-Bound Angels. I am an Earth-Bound Angel. Spirits come to me with their messages. Why was I so afraid of them? Could my father be right that it was just not my time for my "awakening?" Did fate manipulate my coming here to the new house so I would be here when Johnny died? Could it have something to do with how or why he was killed? My mother spoke of a bigger plan that could have included our moving and Johnny's death. Could my meeting with his friends today be part of that plan? I pull out the photograph to study his expression – and Maggie's.

Chapter 10

It's three thirty pm and my father comes to my room to tell me he's leaving to go to the police station. He wishes me luck with the neighborhood kids and I wish him luck with the police. I almost say I want to go with him to talk along the way, but my mother is standing with him staring at me strangely. I know she wants time with me. When he turns and leaves, she walks over to my bed.

"Can we talk?" she asks.

"Sure," I answer.

"Your father said he spoke with you."

"Yes," I say.

"And you read the emails?"

"Yes. Some of them." I look up at her and smile. "Did he really ask you to squeeze his hand to see if he was dreaming?"

She giggles; it is something I have never seen her do. I try to picture her as a young girl. It isn't hard. Her freckles still jump when she speaks just as my father described them.

"Your father was quite a character when I met him," she said. "I couldn't believe he had the 'gift'. It was as if it was all meant to be. There really is no such thing as coincidence."

"Do you believe that everything that happened was supposed to happen? Did we move here because Johnny needs me?"

"I couldn't tell you that for sure, but if you're asking me if that's what *I* believe, then yes. Somehow you were predestined to be here at the precise time Johnny was killed. I also suppose you'll get more answers today when you meet his friends."

I look at her for a moment trying to comprehend what she has just said and contemplate telling her about Maggie's picture; I decide against it for now. "Do you think Johnny's friends are Earth-Bound Angels? Do you think Maggie is?"

"I don't know what to think. I only know that you'll find out soon enough and whatever is intended to happen, will happen. The real question is whether you're willing to take on whatever task you're asked to do."

I look at her and try to gather my thoughts.

"Are you?" she asks.

"I think I am," I hear myself say. "I saw Johnny in a dream and he pointed to a photo of himself with Maggie."

She looks at me surprised. "He's already started to

communicate with you. Listen carefully to everything he says and does. Every detail has importance."

"Is that why it's important to read Dad's emails? Will learning about Melinda help me to understand how they communicate with us?"

She gives me a wide smile."Melinda's story is your father's story. It shows how things went for your father on his first save. You need to get a good sense of the importance of what you're being asked to do. This is not a game, Peter. Earth-Bound Angels are a part of life and death. The souls that you're helping could be trapped in limbo forever without you. You're their chance for eternal peace and very well may be their last opportunity to reach the Light. Being an Earth-Bound truly is a gift and your father and I are very proud of what we are. We hope you will be, too."

"Did you have a first save, too? Is that in here?" I hold up the emails.

"No. Let's save that story for another time. You have more than you can handle already."

She reaches over and kisses my forehead and says, "Keep reading and listening, but remember, you have an appointment at six."

I stare after her as she leaves and then search quickly through the pages to find more on Melinda and my father's mission.

TO: *Paranormalinsite2@email.com*
FROM: *DamienDarrk@info.org*

The girl in my closet, Melinda, did not come here until one year after my father's accident. Did he send her? Is he talking through her? Can he talk through you? Why is it taking him so long to reach me? Can you interpret dreams from the Other Side?

My father said there are many people who say they hear voices. They write books and movies and give lectures, but are not truly connected. Why am I not connecting to you?

Do spirits have frequencies? Are they like radio waves that seek receivers? How do the undead reconnect with the living? How do they choose their listeners and reach those of us who want to listen?

Exactly! I say to myself. How do they choose their listeners and reach those who want to listen? How and why did Johnny pick me? What can I do for him that other Earth-Bounds can't do? What ways will he choose to communicate with me?

My dreams have been taken over by Melinda.

There are no nights now when she doesn't come to me.
She comes out of her closet a mass of energy floating
until I am pushed into my dreams. Some dreams are too
real. And then they make no sense. They change so
quickly. In them I see Melinda. The man at the swings
comes back in shadows. Is the sad man my father and
the crying Melinda me?

I'm confused by his dreams and almost want to force myself to sleep so I can have dreams of my own. Communications with Johnny. I skim to an email explaining where the police have given my father information about my grandfather. They tell him that his father had a gift for him among his possessions.

TO: Paranormalinsite2@email.com
FROM: DamienDarrk@info.org

They told us where the car had been taken and
gave us two boxes. One had all of his personal
belongings, his clothes and wallet and jewelry. The other
was smaller than a breadbox wrapped in colorful paper
with a bow and card that said Happy Birthday Son.
The present is still in my closet with Melinda. It is
in one corner and she is in the other. I refuse to open it

until he says I can.

The present? A gift? My grandfather had a gift for my father? What did he bring him? I search my memory for mentions of the gift and remember that he talked about it after his father's burial service at the cemetery. He rushed home after hearing the voices in the cemetery!

The light was on when I returned home. My mother was sleeping in a chair. I went to my room and stood for a long time staring at my closet door waiting for him to speak to me. My father's present was sitting in there where my mother had placed it and there were no sounds from the closet—until my birthday—one year later.

He let the box stay in his closet for a whole year? How could it not make him crazy? What could his father have left for him?

Ice, then fire. When I reached for the box I felt her energy sliding first across the back of my hand and then up my arm into my neck and shoulders. A chill ran through me, then comfort. I have never tried to touch the box since. Can the things people touch before they

die carry a piece of their souls? Can they carry messages
we are meant to understand?

I reach under my mattress and touch the photo of Maggie and Johnny. Nothing happens and I continue reading.

What will our spirits look like when we return? Will
we look the way we did at the time of our death? Will we
resemble who we were or be floating masses of
shapeless energy only visible on this side in dreams and
visions that must be interpreted?

I try to analyze my father's questions. How do the dead communicate with the living? Johnny appeared to me as himself at the accident, not a floating mass of shapeless energy. Not speaking. Then he came as just a voice in my room. And then appeared in my doorway and later in my dreams pointing to a photo of Maggie. *"Can the things people touch before they die carry a piece of their souls? Can they carry messages we're meant to understand?"* My father first experienced Melinda in his closet. Moaning and whining. Later she made physical contact and used dreams to communicate a story of a man at a bridge. "Do they come in dreams and visions that must be interpreted?" Again I turn to Melinda, my father, and the paranormal to study how she communicated.

79

I know my father is trying to reach me. I feel his presence and I know the key is Melinda. She is still in my closet across the corner from his present. She has become more daring. She moans and whines less and appears to me more often. Still hovering, watching, floating, rubbing up against me wearing my body like an old suit. And the dreams haven't stopped. She comes to me in them every night with her pink ribbon bouncing and the handsome man in the shadows constantly around her, watching her. And me.

The email ends there and I sit here thinking. Can I force myself to sleep so he'll be able to contact me?

I attempt to read again, but I'm interrupted by my mother.

"Peter? It's nearly six o' clock. Maggie and her friends are expecting you."

Chapter 11

It is five thirty. I have almost made myself late. I search
frantically for something to wear and think about what they were
wearing when they visited. I choose a black shirt and black pants,
slip on black boots, and run a brush quickly through my hair.

"I'm not sure what time I'll be back," I shout from my
bathroom.

My mother rushes over to me with a ten dollar bill. "You
should get yourself a slice of pizza or something in case you're
running late. Would you like me to drive you there?"

"It's not far," I say.

A light, small flurry blows around me reminding me of the
squalls that followed us here. I pull up my collar and rush down
Dexter away from my house and Johnny's. A couple of cars pass
me as I hurry down the sidewalk. A woman stares at me from the
front porch of one of the smaller houses. My head is spinning as I
hurry along and before I know it, I'm facing the pizzeria – and

Maggie. Her face is red and she has obviously been standing on the corner by the pillars for awhile.

"You're seven minutes late," she says.

Across the street through the large glass window I can see Luke and Paul watching us.

"Why did you come here?" she asks.

"What?"

"Did he send you?"

I stare into her face and she stares back as if she is trying to see my soul. I have no idea what to say to her.

"Okay, are you one of *them*?"

I'm almost ready to ask her if she means an Earth-Bound Angel, but she continues talking. "I need to know if you're one of them or one of us."

I continue staring with nothing to say.

"You don't have to tell me," she says. "We'll find out sooner or later. If you lie to us, we'll know."

"I don't know what you're talking about," I manage to say.

"I suppose it's a coincidence that you have long hair like us and wear black? If it's just to pretend you're one of us it won't work. Give up now or I promise you'll be sorry."

"Listen," I tell her. "I've had long hair since I was six years old. I can show you pictures."

She stares at me long and hard. "When?" she asks.

"When what?" I answer.

"When can you show me the pictures?"

"Whenever," I say, "you can come to my house. My mother has them somewhere and I can show them to you."

"What are you doing tomorrow morning?" she asks.

"I guess showing you pictures of me at my house," I say.

She smiles and says, "Okay. I'm coming over tomorrow. We'll figure out a time."

I want to melt when I see her smile because it is so amazing, and then I remember what she looked like in the photo with Johnny. She's not smiling in the photo. I gear up to ask her if she was his girlfriend, but she doesn't give me time to ask. "Okay, I'm going to take a chance on you. Come in to the pizzeria with me. We need to talk."

The snow is heavier and it has gotten colder, but the pizzeria is warm and comfortable and smells great. The three boys are sitting now and looking at me as if they're doing some sort of inspection. There's a large pizza on the table with two slices missing and Luke offers a slice to me. I hesitate and he says, "Go ahead. We already ate a whole one."

"We get them for half price," Mark says, and Luke gives him a dirty look.

"Go ahead and have a slice," Luke says. "It's the best pizza anywhere around."

He hands me a slice and Paul pulls out a chair for me. I sit in it and take a bite; Luke is right. It's the best pizza I've ever tasted.

"It's really good," I say and take another bite, which is definitely the best thing I could have done because they are all smiling. I look over at the guy behind the counter who is staring at me waiting for a response. I give him a "thumbs-up" and he gives me one back, then gets back to work making more pizzas.

"Are you a Disciple?" Luke asks. "Don't give us any bull. Just tell me straight. Did they get to you?"

I am about to bite my slice of pizza again and freeze with my mouth still open.

"Just say yes or no," Paul says.

"I told you we'll find out either way. Are you, or have you ever been, a Disciple? Did they put you up to coming here tonight? Answer the question, Peter," Maggie demands.

"I came because *you* invited me."

"But are you a Disciple or intend to be?"

"I'm not sure," I manage to say.

Wrong answer. Maggie jumps up and throws her hands in the air and Paul slams his hand on the table.

"How can you not be sure?" Maggie asks. "You either are or you aren't. You were or you weren't. You want to be or you don't."

Just as I am about to ask if an Earth-Bound Angel is a Disciple, Paul asks, "Do you belong to the Disciples; are you considering joining them?"

"Is that some kind of school club or gang from here that I'm supposed to know? Because I've only lived here for a day. I never belonged to any clubs at home. We didn't even have gangs. You're the first people from the school I've even met. I was in the glee club for less than a week at home and quit. I lived in the mountains."

They all stare at me and Maggie says, "Glee Club?" and cracks up laughing. I am too confused to laugh with her. She looks at the others and says, "I think he's telling the truth." She looks at me and says, "The Disciples are a group of students at our school and are our enemies. They hate the fact that we have long hair and dress in black; they hate *us*. We hate *them* even more. They don't like what we do and we definitely don't like what they do."

"What do they do?" I ask.

They all look at each other and sort of shrug their shoulders.

Luke says, "Smoke pot, have parties and cause trouble, mostly for us. They call us every name in the book and accuse us of being everything we're not." He stops talking and looks at me closely. "Did you always have long hair? Are you telling me you

85

just decided to wear black by coincidence tonight? That just seems too weird to be true."

"I may have been influenced by the fact that you were all wearing black when you came to my house. I guess I figured black was in around here." I pause. "Or maybe I thought I should wear black because of what happened to Johnny."

Luke jumps from his seat and grabs me by my shirt scaring the crap out of me. "Don't use Johnny as an excuse. You didn't even know Johnny. If you really knew him you'd bow your head when you said his name. I don't care what the others say. I don't think you can be trusted."

"Look, I didn't mean anything by it---"

"He didn't, "Maggie said. "He just moved in. I think we should tell him what things are like around here and let him decide what side he wants to be on. Let him meet the Disciples." She looks me straight in the eyes and says, "If you have half a brain, you'll keep wearing black clothes and long hair and stick with us," she stops for a second, "and just to be sure Luke is not right about you, I'm still coming over to your house tomorrow morning to see those pictures of you. Right now we have a lot of work to do to get ready for the candle vigil. If you still want to help we can use it."

"I'm in," I said. "What can I do?"

Luke looks over at Maggie who is now seated next to me

and it has suddenly become a meeting. We discuss Johnny's plan to "put a candle in every window on Christmas Eve" as a symbol of peace and the coming of The Savior. They tell me that Johnny was a savior himself and he wanted to change the world – until the world changed him.

"It wasn't the *world* that changed him," Paul growls, "it was---" all eyes go to him and he stops talking immediately.

"We already have the candles," Maggie says. "We bought them with money we raised and the church helped us to get them. We were going to give them out at church on Christmas Eve but now we need to organize it around the wake and funeral."

"We're all meeting at the funeral parlor tomorrow at one thirty. The services are at two. My father knows the funeral director and he said we can give out the candles then and ask people to light them on Christmas Eve as a remembrance to Johnny. Almost everyone in Starlight will be there. His parents said Johnny would really like that. You can join us if you want."

"Sure," I say.

"I still want to see those pictures," Maggie says. "Tomorrow morning at ten?"

"Sure," I say again.

She walks me to the door and then out to the sidewalk.

I stand staring at her and she looks me straight in the eyes. "I know he sent for you," she says.

"I told you I never heard of the Disciples," I tell her.

"I'm not talking about the Disciples," she says. "I'm talking about Johnny."

She turns and walks away and I'm left staring after her until I finally make my way home. The minute I enter the house, my parents are standing in front of me, questioningly.

"How did it go my father asks?"

"Weird," I say. "I think Maggie could be an Earth-Bound."

My parents glance at each other quickly."Why would you say that?" my mother asks.

"The last thing she said to me was that she knows Johnny sent for me."

"That could just be because you got here when you did."

"Maybe," I say, and turn to my father. "How did it go at the police station?"

"There are still a lot of unanswered questions. They're performing an autopsy to see if they can put together a scenario of exactly what happened, but I think we should talk about Johnny and his friends. Do you know anything about James and Judis?"

"Who?" I ask.

"Evidently, you haven't met them yet. They hang around with Johnny or did hang around with Johnny until this all happened. They're considered 'Persons of Interest' in the accident. It seems I'm not the only one who mentioned a car with one headlight being at the scene of the accident. Apparently, this James kid has a car with one headlight. There's also something going on with a rival group of kids at the school called 'Disciples'."

"They talked about them today," I say. "Do they have anything to do with Earth-Bound Angels?" I ask.

My mother jumps in and says, "It may seem like a coincidence, but there's a group of Earth-Bounds who call themselves Disciples. They aren't exactly like us."

"They're more like Earth-Bound *Demons*," my father says. "Your mother and I have both run into them a few times. They "save" tortured souls from limbo too, only they don't steer them into the Light."

"They steer them into hell?" I ask.

"Let's just say they don't steer them into the Light," my father says. "It's best you keep your distance from them. Are you comfortable enough with Johnny's friends to hang out with them for awhile until you get the feel for things around here?"

"I guess," I say. "Maggie is coming here in the morning."

My mother raises her eyebrows and says, "Just Maggie? Not the boys?"

"She's coming to see our old family pictures. Can you help me find them?"

She raises her eyebrows again and makes a "nice job"

kind of face and I tell her to cut it out. My father laughs and makes the same kind of face.

"I'm going to my room to read," I say.

Chapter 12

Once I'm in the room, I reach under my mattress to pull out the picture of Johnny and Maggie and something begins to happen. A crazy kind of tingling in my fingers starts climbing through the back of my hand and up my arm. I freak out and drop the frame to the floor. As I bend to pick it up, I see a long crack down the middle of the glass separating Maggie from Johnny.

I have goose bumps on my arms and legs. When I look at the manuscript it has mysteriously flipped to another page about Melinda. I pull myself up to the head of my bed and rest myself against my pillows as I begin reading.

Melinda's dreams are sometimes so frightening I wake up unable to breathe. I'm in them being warned and I'm trying to understand her but I can't. I scream at her to make sense but she doesn't. The man in the shadows is in the dreams too. He is laughing at first and when Melinda talks to me and I don't understand her he stops laughing and begins whining. And I wake up to the noises in my closet.

I dreamt of her one night when the man wasn't there. And it was as if she was someone else. We were alone and her blue eyes paralyzed me, pulled me inside out. And when she said LET GO and I did, I began falling at an incredible speed. I was falling faster, and faster, with each second. The fear building inside of me. Frantically, I searched for something to grab, something to break my fall. And there were hands attached to corpses. Hundreds of naked bodies from photos I had seen somewhere. I wanted to turn from them but I needed them to catch me. To stop me from falling. And I screamed for them to please help me but my mother came instead and asked me if I was having a bad dream.

"Yes," I said.

My heart nearly beats through my chest. What is that supposed to mean? Were the corpses Earth-Angels of some sort trying to save him from falling? Or Disciples? Did my father have a dream about Disciples of Darkness reaching out to him? I thumb ahead quickly and Melinda's story continues in a dream.

Melinda was at the wooden bridge crying and the man from the shadows was standing over her. The man reached out his hand and Melinda pulled away. He reached for her and she tried to run but the railing gave way. I heard myself scream. I wanted to reach for her to save her. I could see her falling down faster and faster and the corpses' hands were reaching out to catch her but they couldn't and my mother's voice interrupted again asking me if I was having another bad dream.

The railing gave way and she fell! Were the corpses *after* her or *helping* her? Were they *Disciples* trying to catch her from falling? I search for the next email.

I was still awake when the sun came up; her whimpering would not let me sleep and she had entered me somehow. I could feel her wearing me, writhing under my skin trying to find a place to be safe. And then she was hovering above me. I looked up at her and she smiled and then I saw something strange in the center of her hazel eyes.

I reach for the photo and am almost afraid to look at it. When I do, Maggie's hazel eyes are staring back at me. I turn quickly from them and return to Melinda's story.

That night Melinda spoke to me. She hovered over my bed and when I opened my eyes hers were staring into mine. "You mustn't fear the voices," she said. "Go to the cemetery."

I awoke as I usually do from dreams like that, cold and sweaty. My room was totally silent. I looked at my closet and stared through the darkness, then got up from my bed. When I went to open my closet door it opened by itself. I could barely breathe. I thought for sure my mother would be knocking at the door. My heartbeat seemed almost deafening. Slowly, I fell to my knees, and as I reached for my father's present, Melinda did as she had done before. She entered me through my hand and climbed through me slowly until every part of me was filled with her.

I stayed on my knees for what seemed to be hours frozen to the spot and a dream passed through me as if each of the thoughts in the dream were mine. Melinda was with the man from the shadows but now his face was clear. He was holding Melinda's hand and they were standing by a grave-stone looking out toward the gate.

They turned to each other and the same dream I had before began to play again. Melinda was at the wooden bridge crying and the man from the shadows was standing over her. The man reached out his hand and Melinda pulled away. I heard myself screaming. I wanted to reach for her to save her. I could see her falling down faster and faster and the corpses' hands were reaching out to catch her but they couldn't. And my mother's voice asked me again if I was having another bad dream. Her hand touched my shoulders from behind me and I jumped when I felt her. I thought she was Melinda.

She helped me to my feet and led me to my bed then sat beside me.

"Do you hear the voices?" she asked. "Is someone in your closet? Has your father come back?"

"No," I said.

"I haven't heard from him yet."

"I thought you might hear the voices the way he did," she said

"You knew about his voices?" I asked.

"Yes," she said. "But I never let him talk about them."

"Were you afraid of them?" I asked.

"Terrified," she said. "I thought if he told me about them they would start visiting me and I knew I couldn't handle it."

"Are you still afraid? I asked.

"I am still mortified. But I want you to tell me everything."

We sat until the sun came up and I didn't miss a detail. I read her every email I've written to you. When I was done she said I should sleep for awhile, and then we should go together to the cemetery.

Chapter 13

I try to make sense of what I've read. Melinda was using my father's dreams to lead him to the cemetery. My grandmother was going to face her fears and take him there. But why is Melinda taking them there? Doesn't she know he hears their voices?

My mother was sitting at the table fully dressed and ready and so was I. We got into the car without talking and drove straight to the cemetery gate. As we approached, I felt myself shaking. I wanted to run from the car but she was there inside of me, forcing me to continue on. I held my breath and listened for the deluge, but nothing came.

My mother looked at me as if to say, "Are you okay?"

"I don't hear them," I said. "I think Melinda asked them not to speak. She doesn't want me to be afraid and is with me."

"And I'm sure," my mother said, "that your father is with us too."

She pulled bravely to the side of the little road and turned off the engine. We went to his stone. I expected to hear his voice then and begged him to say something. But there was silence. My body began to move without me. I walked as my mother followed to a stone near my father's grave, and my mother gasped. The stone read, "Rest In Peace – Melinda Johnson Age 9" and my skin began to tingle. No, burn. And I wanted to run but my feet were anchored to her grave site.

When my feet were free to move again they went to the stone next to Melinda's. I could see his sad face in my mind as clearly as it had appeared in my dream and then I heard the weeping. My mother was crying.

"I know this story," she said. "It happened over 20 years ago right after we moved in. It was heartbreaking."

The whining was deafening. It came from inside of me and then became a whimper as my mother told the story that had once made the headlines of a man who had killed his daughter and himself rather than lose his family to divorce.

What? I couldn't believe what I was reading. They all

thought that Melinda's father killed her? It was an accident! The railing gave way! Is that why she was haunting my father? She needed to set the story straight? I had to keep reading!

"She's still alive," I heard myself shout. "She's talking to me."

My mother stared at me in disbelief. "Melinda?" she asked. "It can't be."

"No, "I shouted again. "Melinda is saying her mother is still alive."

My mother put her hands to her mouth and through her tears she said, "We must go there. I know where she lives."

I bent before my father's grave and kissed it before going to the car. As the engine started I heard a slow murmur. It began to rise and get louder. They were starting to talk! All of them at once and I begged my mother to hurry out of the cemetery gates.

My bones have turned to ice. He's hearing the voices and they're surrounding him as he hurries out of the cemetery. But where are they going? Part of me is begging me to continue, but another part is demanding that I put the emails away. It's telling me to lie back on my bed. To go to sleep. But I'm not tired. Still, I find myself getting out of my clothes and back into bed. It is nine thirty pm.

The next thing I see is a swing set and a man running from the bridge. There is a girl against the railing. She is trying to get away from the man but the railing breaks and they are falling. I run to them and am standing close to them now. I can see their faces; the man is Johnny and he is trying to keep Maggie from falling into the hands of the naked corpses!

Chapter 14

It is now ten fifteen. I am sitting up in bed in a cold sweat. *"Do they come in dreams and visions that must be interpreted?"*

Slowly, I step out of bed and work my way to the living room; my father is watching TV and my mother has already gone to bed. He looks at me and says, "A dream?"

"Yes," I say.

"Can I help?"

"I think so," I tell him. "Do you remember in your dream when Melinda falls with her father from the bridge?"

"You are almost at the end of the book," he says.

"Yes," I answer. "Do you remember all the hands of the corpses trying to save them from falling? Are they Earth-Bound Angels trying to save them from falling to the depths, or Disciples trying to lead them there?"

He smiles. "That's a great question. Did you dream about them, too?"

"Yes. Only it wasn't Melinda and her father who were falling; it was Johnny and Maggie. What does it mean?"

"To be honest, I'm not sure. I suspect that Maggie is in some sort of danger. Johnny is reaching out to save her from falling into the depths. I imagine he needs you to help her. Did you say you were seeing her tomorrow?"

"Yes," I say.

"Good. I expect you'll get some answers from her then. You'd better get some sleep. It sounds like you're going to need it."

"Should I try to read the last of your emails to make myself sleepy?"

He makes a weird face and says, "My writing puts you to sleep?"

"No, I mean---"

"I'm kidding," he says. "How far did you get?"

"You and your mother are leaving the cemetery to go somewhere."

"Read a little more and find out what Melinda's true story is. You're in for a few surprises."

"Okay," I say. As I leave, I turn back to him. "Thanks for your help."

"Are you okay with all of this?" he asks.

"I'm okay with it," I say. "I just want to know what it all

means."

"Me too," he says. "I'm sure you'll know very soon."

When I get to my bed I grab for his emails and fumble through the pages trying to find where I left off. Frantically, I shuffle through the pages and finally find my place.

The house was less than two blocks from ours, unkempt and sorrowful. My insides were ready to explode and I wanted desperately to leave but I knew I couldn't. I had to take her in there and tell her mother the truth about Melinda and the accident. My mother rang the bell and an old woman stood before us.

"Are you Mrs. Johnson?" my mother asked.

The whining inside of me became a painful whimpering.

"No," the woman said.

And my mother and I stood there confused and speechless.

"What do you want of her?" the woman asked "She is not well."

My mother lied and said we were old friends making a Sunday visit. The woman was skeptical but allowed us into the bedroom where Melinda's mother lay dying. I began to cry as I saw her frail body.

"Are you death?" she asked. "I thought you'd be

bigger," she said and attempted a smile.

"My son has a special gift," my mother said.

"You needn't tell me why you've come," she answered. "I have always known it was an accident. And I knew she would find a way to bring me peace. Bring her to me."

I walked closer to the bed and it was as if Melinda began electrocuting me. The woman took my hand in hers and Melinda flowed through me with a force that drained me of my strength. Both her mother and I fought desperately to keep breathing.

I sit on my bed in disbelief trying disparagingly to keep my own breath. Melinda has not only entered his body but has allowed him to transport her to her mother's bedside. And he has transferred her to her mother!

My mother was terrified and sobbed loudly as the woman's eyes closed. She was smiling, motionless and peaceful. Dead-like. And then her eyes jerked open. Her voice was weak and barely audible.

"We have something for you," she whispered. She pointed to her night stand and there, exactly as I had remembered it, was the pink ribbon Melinda had worn in my dreams.

I let go of the woman's hand and took the ribbon.

"May you both have peace," I said.

She took my hand in both of hers. "And may your own entry into the Light be as peaceful and joyful as you have made the possibility of ours."

Then we were dismissed. The other woman walked us to the door and said, "My sister knew you would come some day. She waited patiently and painfully. God bless you for bringing my niece home to us. Your reward will be in a better world."

I am breathless again. My father was able to release her soul from his closet and bring her home to her mother who had been waiting and suffering for nearly a lifetime. I struggle to catch my breath, wipe my eyes, and begin reading.

When we got into the car I felt strange. Empty but happy. I turned to say something to my mother who was crying. "I should have been more understanding," she said. "I should have shared these moments with your father."

When we got into the house I went directly to my room and opened the closet door. Melinda was not there of course. I reached into my pocket, took out the pink ribbon, and placed it in her corner. But before I shut the

door, I checked for the box with my father's present to
me.

The email ends there. I set the pile down and run out to my father. "What was in the present?" I ask.

He jumps at the sudden sound of my voice and then begins to laugh. "Do you honestly think I'm going to tell you?" he asks.

"Can't you just tell me what he gave you?" I ask.

"Can't you just read it?" he answers.

I hurry back to my room without answering him and pick up where I left off.

TO: Paranormalinsite2@email.com
FROM: DamienDarrk@info.org

There were sixty-three emails from Katie so I invited her to come over. Two minutes after I pressed "send" the phone rang.

"This better be good," she said.

"You won't believe how good it is," I said. "Can you come over right now?"

"I'm almost there," she said.

I went downstairs to thank my mother for coming with me. She was sitting in my father's chair with his picture in her lap.

"I miss him so much," she said. "I would give

106

anything to see those hazel eyes alive again."

Hazel eyes. So I have my grandfather's eyes as well as his gift.

"Katie is coming over," I said. "I want to open Dad's present and can't do it alone. I want to open it with the two of you.

I am so buried in the story that I barely hear the light tap on my door.

"Come in," I say. My father enters.

Chapter 15

"Did you find out what the present was?" he asks.

"No," I say. "I was interrupted."

"Oops. Sorry," he says, and turns to go; I stop him.

"You brought Melinda to her mother so they could be at peace? Did your father go to the Light with them?"

He smiles. "You'll have to read that for yourself. It's only a few more pages. But I suggest you wait until the morning. You're going to need your sleep."

"So does all of this mean Johnny needs me so he can cross over?"

"That's what I thought originally, but there may be more to it. I'm afraid you're going to have to let it all play out to get the answers."

"Do you think I'll dream about him tonight?"

"Not if you don't go to sleep," he says. "Good night."

Before he leaves, I say, "Dad, I love you."

"I love you too," he says. "Let me know in the morning if you've had any more dreams."

I lie in my bed thinking about all that I've read, trying to anticipate the ending of his book and wondering what it will be like with Maggie in the morning.

At five thirty-two I wake up and sit upright in my bed, surprised that I had fallen asleep. I try to remember if I had any dreams. There are none I can remember. I look around quickly to see if anything has changed. Everything is where I left it, including my father's emails. I grab them up, take a deep breath, and prepare to read the ending of his story.

TO: *Paranormalinsite2@email.com*
FROM: DamienDarrk@info.org

Katie came with her mother and my mother asked if we should go to my room. "Not yet," I said.

"Is there something wrong," Katie asked

"No," I said. "I have something to tell you."

We sat on my bed and I started at the beginning the way I did with my mother. Before I knew it she was sitting there wide-eyed and crying.

"I love what you can do," she said. "And I love what you did for Melinda."

"Are you frightened by my ability to talk with

them?"

"Not even a little," she said.

"I think it's wonderful that you can speak to them. And I want to read your emails."

"Some of them are about you," I said.

"They'd better be good things," she warned.

"There is nothing bad about you," I answered.

She leaned into me and I kissed her on the lips. The tingling started somewhere inside me and for a moment I thought Melinda had returned. But then recognized it as my own heat rising. We kissed again and my mother interrupted us.

"Is it time?" she asked

"For what?" Katie asked back.

I told her my father brought a gift for me the day he died. When I spoke with him the day before he said it was something special.

"Is it smaller than a breadbox," I asked.

"Yes," he said, but much more meaningful.

I told her I hadn't opened it yet. Would she like to open it with me.

"Oh my God, yes!" she said

Oh my God, yes! I say out loud. *Please* open it!

Katie's mother was still in the room and I let her stay. I knew my father wouldn't mind. I didn't want to be alone. All of their eyes were on me as I brought the gift to the bed. My hands were shaking. It was heavier than I remembered. I removed the card and untaped the paper slowly. Too slowly for Katie and our mothers. They looked like they were going to tear it out of my hands. And then it was opened.

They were hand-written books. I opened the envelope and read the card.

Dear Son,

If you are reading this, I am already gone. I would have taken this card off the box if I was wrong about my premonition. I am afraid of what may happen today but can do nothing to stop it.

I suspect that my dream has become a reality. Your mother and your new friends surround you but I don't know how much time has passed. I wish I could have been there but I have been called to where I was destined to be. I suspect that all I anticipated about Melinda has already happened. They have probably arrived here. Well done if it is so.

It is my hope that she is the first of

111

many souls you will save. But you will not do it alone. If you have not met her yet, you will. She too is an Earth-Bound Angel. It is your fate to be with her. Recognize her by the color of my eyes and by the gift she will develop.

I looked up at Katie and she was smiling.

"It started when I was fourteen," she said, "but I've kept it secret."

I stared at her in disbelief and then continued to read his letter.

Note that I have written most of this in diary poems. It is an art I've learned to master and had hoped to teach you how to write them someday. You will find many more in the books I've written for you.

"Wait," I say aloud. "My grandfather wrote in Diary Poems? Where are they? What did he say in them?" The email ends and a new one begins.

TO: Paranormalinsite2@email.com
FROM: DamienDarrk@info.org

His diary poems were the most amazing things I

112

had ever seen. They were written in ten line verses with ten verses to a section and three sections to a chapter. In them were his thoughts and experiences of all the souls he had encountered through his lifetime. They are his questions and his answers about the After-life.

I want to run out to my father to ask him where those poems are, but it is only six o' clock in the morning and I am nearly finished with his emails. I need to continue.

I know now why I couldn't reach him. His many years of soul-saving earned him his immediate "Right of Passage" to the Light, beyond the troubled souls and the ability to communicate, a right that I hope to earn someday.

Chapter 16

I was right about my grandfather going directly to the Light, but I'm troubled by what it may mean. My mother and father are trying to earn their way directly to the Light too. If they succeed and pass before I do, will I lose the ability to communicate with them? I go quickly back to the reading to see if my grandfather was able to finally contact my father.

My father said he would love to take credit for Katie but she was always meant to be with me. We are destined for greatness. His poems will guide us into sharing and understanding the purpose of life on earth and in limbo in a time for living and loving, for repenting and dying, and for eternal peace.

There are no insignificant people and no such thing as coincidence. All that happened to me, and will happen to me, is in the books. It has always been. We must accept the essence of who we are and who we must be.

The night we opened the gift we received two phone calls: Mrs. Johnson died peacefully in her sleep. There would be no wake or open casket or visiting hours. She was content to have lived a full life and grateful to be reunited with her loved ones. The second call was from Katie, "Am I upset that I am destined to be with her?"

"Yes," I said. "Just kidding."

"Not funny," she said, "and guess what. I got a call from my father who is sending me a ticket to come visit him. I haven't seen him since he left us. I'm going to go for a week sometime after the dance."

TO: *Paranormalinsite2@email.com*
FROM: *DamienDarrk@info.org*

I don't know if you will ever read these, but my writing them has brought focus and importance to my life. I said when I began writing to you that I believed dead people live here. I know now they do. I said I was helpless without you. I'm not. Perhaps someday our paths will cross and I can thank you for what you have helped me to do. In the meantime, I have a tux to rent *and a limo to share with the geeks, George, Eric, and Todd.*

By the way, I had a dream the night we opened my father's gift. Melinda's father was at the bridge and Melinda came to him and smiled. They turned together holding hands and were suddenly standing at a stone in the cemetery. They were looking out at the gate waiting for someone. And then her mother came to join them. There was another person in the dream, a man in the shadows. I couldn't see his face, but when he turned to walk into the woods Melinda and her parents followed him and a beautiful bright light appeared. After they walked into it they turned to face me and I saw my father smiling behind them.

His story ends there and I lie with my head in my pillow thinking about Melinda, my father, and my grandfather, and though I fight to stay awake, I can feel myself drifting off.

I am swinging on the swing in the back yard reading my father's manuscript. When I look up, I see someone standing at the bridge. I can't make out who it is at first but I expect it to be Melinda's father, or Johnny. When I walk over, the person turns to face me.

"I know who you are," I say.

"I know who you are, too," he answers. "Have you been

paying attention?"

"I have," I say.

"Do you understand?"

"Some," I say. "There are things that are not clear to me. Are you my guardian angel?"

He laughs a wonderful soft laugh. "No, Peter. I am not your guardian angel, you are. But in many ways I am the path to the Light."

"Is God the Light?"

"Yes, Peter. God is the Light."

"Which God?" I ask. There are a lot of religions on earth. Which one has chosen the correct God?"

"All of them," he answers. "God is the spirit of all that is good. He is the peace that can be found in the soul of every living thing. And life isn't limited to man alone. Your father was right when he told you that life was a symbiotic symphony. The goal is to live in harmony."

"We aren't doing very well with that," I say.

He laughs his wonderful laugh again. "No, mankind is not doing well with that."

"What is it that we're supposed to do?"

"Listen to your soul, Peter. The spirits are always talking and prayer is communication."

"But in what religion do we pray?"

"Communication with God has no specific religion or name. It is a communication from soul to soul. It is a continuing journey to the Light. All religions that teach that are right. Prayer is always the answer."

I look up at him and it's my father; I recognize his voice.

"Dad? I thought you were Grandpa."

"No, it's me," my father says. He is standing by my bed. I look around the room. It's my bedroom and it's daylight.

"You slept late, sleepyhead. It's ten o'clock. Did you dream?"

"Of your father," I say.

He smiles.

"He told me that life is a symbiotic symphony."

"He stole my line," he says. "Did he mention the Disciples of Darkness?"

"What?" I ask.

"You'll need to determine who they are and what part they play in the 'symphony.' In the meantime you'd better get dressed."

"You saved Melinda and her parents and helped them reach the Light."

"It's what we do," he says. "You finished reading the emails?"

"Yes," I answer. "And then fell asleep and dreamt of Grandpa. I guess it's my turn to help save someone," I say.

"I guess it is," he says back. "There's a girl here to see you."

Chapter 17

I jump from my bed and get dressed without washing my face or brushing my teeth. When I get out to the living room she isn't there. She's in the dining room sitting by our "Charlie Brown Christmas Tree."

"Nice tree," she says. Her smile is wonderful and I smile back. Her hair is braided now in one long braid and I hardly recognize her.

"Thanks," I say.

"You should put it out there with Johnny's shrine," she says. "He'd like it."

I walk over to get it and she says, "I didn't mean now." We both laugh and my mother comes into the room with my father.

"These are my parents," I say. "This is Maggie."

She reaches out her hand and my parents shake it in turn.

"It's nice to meet you. Welcome to the neighborhood," Maggie says.

"I'm sorry about the loss of your friend. It must be difficult for you," my father tells her.

"Thank you. It is," Maggie answers.

"Peter tells me you would like to see pictures of his younger years," my mother says. "I put an album out on the dining room table with some orange juice and bagels."

I notice for the first time that the food is there.

"We'll let you two do what you need to do; we'll be in the kitchen if you need anything."

"Your parents are nice," Maggie says when they leave.

"They're parents," I say.

She gives me a "That wasn't very nice" look, and I say, "Okay, *nice* parents."

She smiles. "Let's see those pictures."

She takes a seat at the table, pours herself a glass of orange juice, butters a bagel, then sets the bagel on a plate as she reaches for the picture album. Instead of starting at the beginning, she opens to the middle, and there I am at about thirteen with my long hair and braces.

"You wore braces?" she asks.

"Yeah," I answer. "Until I was fourteen."

"Hmm," she says. "I like you better without them."

I expect her to keep looking through the album but she closes it and looks up at me. "Do you have the photograph?"

I'm not sure what she means and I say, "More than these?"

121

"The one of me and Johnny," she says.

My stomach feels like it has collapsed and I try desperately to remember if I mentioned the photo of them to her.

"He told me about it in my dream last night," she says. "He wants to be sure you took it"

There are chills running through me and I'm dizzy.

"It's not a big deal," she says. "He wanted you to take it. Do you have it?" she asks.

"Yes," I say.

I get up to get it and she says, "We can eat first."

She smiles and I try to smile back. My mind is spinning as I struggle to make sense of everything that is happening here. It's almost as if I'm dreaming, but it's all too real.

After taking a bite of her bagel she wipes her hands, then opens the album again. This time my grandfather is staring back at her. He is sitting with my father who is about fourteen in the photograph.

"We have a lot to do," she says. "Johnny needs us. Get the photo so I can see it, then we'll talk at the shrine."

I get up and go to my room where the photo of them is waiting under my mattress. The door clicks shut behind me and I lean against it. "Is this stuff really happening?" I say aloud, then search the room quickly to be sure Johnny isn't standing with me listening.

I feel even more like I'm dreaming when I touch the photo; a warmth surges through me. It is fortunately a calming warmth and I take a deep breath before opening the door.

She's finished her bagel and stands when I come in with the photo. I give it to her. She glances at it quickly and says nothing about the crack running down the middle. Her eyes fill with tears and she's not ashamed to cry in front me.

Suddenly, she shouts, "THANK YOU, MR. AND MRS. LYNCH," scaring me half to death. They appear in the dining room.

"It was wonderful meeting you," Maggie says. "Will I see you at Johnny's wake today?"

"Of course you will," my father says.

"It won't be at the funeral parlor," she says. "There are so many people coming to his wake, they have to hold it in the church."

"That's quite impressive," my mother says.

"*He* was quite impressive," Maggie answers.

"Is it okay if we take this lovely Christmas tree to Johnny's?" she asks as she points to it.

"It's fine," my father says. "Please do. We can get another."

As I turn to leave, Maggie says, "Put the picture of us back where you had it."

123

I'm surprised she doesn't want to take it to him, but I do what I'm told. As I join her at our front door I look back at my parents and they're both smiling.

Just before we get to Johnny's house, Maggie stops walking and turns to me. "He wasn't my boyfriend. But it doesn't mean we didn't love each other. I think that's what he was trying to tell you with the crack in the glass. He didn't want you to think you were taking advantage of his death by stealing his girlfriend. He was a little weird that way. He was *always* worried about other people's feelings. That's why so many people loved him."

We are at the shrine for less than a minute when a woman comes running out to join us. She stops in front of Maggie, takes the tree from her, and starts crying hysterically. Maggie tries to hug her but the tree is squashed between them; I take it carefully and wait until they're through hugging before setting it down by the roadside. The woman sees the tree on the ground and touches it; then she starts crying and hugging Maggie all over again. I get all teary-eyed and try not to cry with them, but I do, and something starts happening. The warmth I felt when I touched the photograph of Maggie and Johnny comes back, only hotter. I want to shout, "Oh, my God, Johnny's inside of me," but I stop myself.

Johnny's mother turns to face me, stares into my eyes, then puts her arms around me. I hug her like I've known her my whole life. The warm feeling soars through me.

"You must be the new boy next door," she says. "I wish you could have met him. You would have loved him. Everybody did." She turns to Maggie. "Will you be coming this afternoon with your parents? Did you get the message that the wake was moved to the church?"

"Yes," Maggie says. "My whole family's coming."

"He loved you so much," she tells her. "Please keep visiting here. I can't bear to lose you both."

"I'll visit often," Maggie says. "I promise."

His mother turns to me and says, "Please stop by the church today and bring your parents. I would love to meet them." She looks at me and starts hugging me again. The warm feeling starts getting hotter.

"I will," I manage to say.

Finally, she turns to leave. My temperature returns to normal as Maggie walks her back to her house.

"Good job," she says to me when she returns.

I get up the courage to ask her outright,"Are you an Earth-Bound?"

"No," she answers. "Just sensitive."

I know I must look confused because she says, "I can communicate with spirits and I feel their presence, but I don't save souls the way you and Johnny and your parents can."

"You know about Earth-Bounds?" I ask.

125

"Johnny was one," she says. "He talked to me about all of his experiences. He told me about you in a dream and said you would be coming here. He said I should help you to do what you need to do."

When we get to my front door, she says, "I need to get ready for the wake."

"I can walk you home," I say.

"No, you need to get ready, too. Wear black. Are you going to help pass out the candles to the people who attend?"

"Of course," I say.

"It starts at two but we're all getting there by one-thirty."

"I can do that," I tell her.

She jogs away from me and I watch her get further and further away until she's gone. When I turn to go into the house, I feel like something is drawing me to Johnny's shrine. I walk slowly toward his house, and when I get there the weird warm feeling comes over me again and it feels like electric waves are passing through me. Then the feeling disappears as quickly as it came.

"I know you used me to hug your mother," I say to Johnny "and I'm willing to do whatever it is you need me to do." I expect him to answer somehow, but he doesn't. After a deep breath, I say, "What is it you want?" Still nothing happens and I turn to walk back to my house. Out of the corner of my eye, I can tell someone's watching me from one of Johnny's windows. I turn slowly to get a better look. The curtain is pulled back and there with his Mona Lisa smile is Johnny.

My mother and father are eating bagels at the dining room table when I go inside.

"It all keeps getting weirder and weirder," I tell them.

"Does that bother you?" my father asks.

"It makes me kind of crazy," I say. "I never know what's coming next."

"We'll help you the best we can," my mother says, "but we don't have any control over what's happening."

I turn to my father. "Maggie says she isn't an Earth-Bound."

"What did she say she was?"

"She said she was 'sensitive'. She can communicate with spirits and feel their presence but she can't save souls the way we can."

"That makes sense," my mother says. "Most people are sensitive to the spirits but they're afraid of them and ignore them. Johnny's probably been helping her to raise her sensitivity and taught her how to connect."

I tell my parents that I think Johnny entered me through the photograph that was at his shrine and got me to bring him here to my room. I said he entered me the way Melinda entered my father so his mother could hug him through me. I also tell them about the break in the glass and that I thought I saw Johnny watching me from a window in his house.

"No two Earth-Bound Angels are the same. Both you and Johnny are different from your father and me. I tried to warn you that you're special, Peter," my mother says. "Your gift is much stronger than your father's or mine, and so is Johnny's evidently. He seems to have amazing powers. We never had spirits appear before us the way he appears to you. I'm sorry this is all happening so quickly for you, but I'm proud of the way you're handling it." She looks at my father. "We both are."

"Well, don't be too proud yet," I say. "I have a feeling there's a lot more to come."

"And I have more than a feeling that you're right," my father says. "Be careful and be alert. Since you have a great potential for doing good, the Disciples will have an even greater reason to keep you from doing it."

"Do you mean the other group of kids from school?"

My father glances at my mother with a "here goes nothing" look on his face. "I'll try to make this as simple as I can for you, Peter. Everything has a purpose and the purpose should *always* be to do good. But that path to good is usually blocked by a desire to do something wrong. Temptation. Your mother and I have names for people who lead us into temptation. We call them

Disciples of Darkness. They distract souls from doing good and lead them away from crossing over to the Light. Eventually, those souls need to depend on Earth-Bound Angels like us to set them free."

He stops talking and looks over at my mother again who gives him a nod of approval. "Your grandfather does a much better job at explaining all of this than I do," he says. He goes over to the bookcase to the right of the fireplace where most of his own books are shelved. "Here," he says," you can read it from the master himself." He takes a worn leather-bound book and sets it face down on the mantel. Dangling from one of its pages is a long pink ribbon.

"Is that Melinda's ribbon?" I ask, amazed.

He smiles. "Yes," he says."These diary poems will tell you a lot of things you want to know, but you don't have time to read them now. Put it back on the mantel until you are ready to read it. We need to get ready to go to Johnny's wake."

"Will Johnny talk to me there?" I ask.

"Frankly, Peter, I have no idea what Johnny will do next," he says.

Chapter 18

It is one fifteen and the church parking lot is already almost full. The church is huge with stone steps leading up to three sets of doors. The center doors are wide-open leading to a vestibule. From the doors there is a clear view of a long aisle to the alter, and at the very end of the aisle is an open coffin. No one is allowed to enter from the center doors and long lines have already formed at both of the side doors. The lines wind down the steps and around both sides of the church. Ushers in suits stand as guards to keep people from entering until it's time to go in.

"I can't believe how many people are already here," my mother says. "Who was this kid?"

"His family has a lot of friends and connections in town," my father says. "Evidently, his father spends a good deal of time at the shooting range with some of his friends on the police force and several local politicians. We'd better get in line. Peter, are you supposed to meet Maggie and the other kids inside?"

"I'm not sure," I say. Right on cue Maggie appears in the center doorway, points to me, and waves me in. I turn to my parents and they say to go ahead; I hurry up the steps and follow her inside to the vestibule where a table is set up with boxes of candles. Luke, Mark and Paul are sitting in chairs ready to work and they all give me a little welcoming wave of their hands. They're wearing black turtleneck shirts and black pants with black boots. Maggie has on a plain black dress and her hair is in a braid again. They stand staring at me. I'm wearing a black suit, black shirt, and a black tie with dress oxfords.

"Let me guess," Maggie says, "that's a designer suit, right?"

"I guess," I say, because I don't dare tell her it's from Brooks Brother's.

She shakes her head and says, "Take a seat. People are already lining up. The family's coming in any minute and Johnny's already up there at the alter. I look up and can see his face sticking up out of the casket. Flowers surround him. I turn away quickly hoping he won't try to communicate with me. A priest is standing by him, and when he sees us, he waves for us to come up to him.

"We have to go up now," Maggie says. "Once they start the lines it will be hours before we get a chance to go up and say a prayer for him."

She leads all of us up the center aisle and, just as we are half-way to the casket, his parents come out from the back of the church to stand by it. Standing right with them, in his Nike sneakers, is *Johnny*.

I turn to Maggie and whisper, "He's here."

"What?" she says.

"Johnny is here by his parents. Can you see him?"

She looks at me as if I've lost my mind.

"He's standing right there next to his mother. Can't you see him?"

She finally looks like she understands and says, "Come here."

I follow her to Johnny's casket and we kneel quickly to say a prayer. I avoid looking at him by closing my eyes; the only thing I pray for is that he won't try to talk to me. Then she takes my arm and brings me to his parents.

Maggie hugs them and they cry together before she introduces me to Johnny's father. All the while I'm concentrating on the Johnny standing there with his Mona Lisa smile. He's looking directly into my eyes and I can barely breathe. His parents say how nice it is that I came to help out with the candles and ask me if we're all settled in yet. I think they ask me more questions but my heart is beating so loudly I can't hear anything they're saying. Finally, I hear them ask if my parents are there.

"They're in line, "I say.

"We're looking forward to meeting them," his father says, and then Maggie turns me away from them to face Johnny!

"*This*," Maggie says. "Is *Frankie*. Johnny's younger brother."

My mind is spinning and I try desperately to make sense of what she has just said. His expression barely changes as he reaches out his hand to shake mine. I'm almost afraid to touch it. He's the spitting image of Johnny.

"I'm sorry about your brother," I manage to say.

"I saw you at our house and yours," he says.

I stand there breathless and staring. I know his voice. It is the one that spoke to me from the glass doors in my bedroom! "You came to my house a couple of times," I say.

"Yes," he answers.

I stand there speechless. Luke nudges me and says, "You have to keep moving."

"You look like you've seen a ghost," Maggie says when we get back to the table. "I guess you didn't know Johnny had a brother."

"He looks exactly like him," I say. "Are they twins?"

"No, Frankie's a year and a half younger, but everyone always took them for twins. He isn't anything like Johnny. He got into trouble a lot and Johnny had to keep bailing him out. He doesn't hang around with us much anymore. I don't know what's going to happen to him now that Johnny's gone. He's been hanging around with James and Judis and he may even be hanging out with the Disciples. You haven't met James and Judis yet, but they're supposed to be coming to help with the candles, if they aren't in jail."

I want to ask her what that means, but the priest has given the signal. People begin to fill the church from the side aisles but stop just short of the casket so the priest can lead everyone in the opening prayer. He tells us that Johnny was not only an important member of the school and town community, but an active member of the church community as well.

"We are gathered here today to pay tribute to a remarkable young man who has found his rightful place with the God he faithfully believed in. I am humbled by the many times I have heard him speak to the members of our church from this very podium. I dare say Johnny was a much better speaker than I am," the priest says. A few people laugh and there is a low mumble as people whisper comments. "There are few here who have not heard him speak for peace in his role as President of the Young Peacemakers Club. He has dutifully and eloquently addressed our congregation, our town, our schools, and even our local and state legislators. The presence here today of the many war veterans whose lunches and dinners he has addressed, and the cadets of

West Point he has spoken to on many occasions, speaks well for their appreciation of this extraordinary young man's ability to captivate an audience. I am sure he would be proud to see how many people he has brought here today.

"As you pay your respects to his family, please be reminded that funeral services will begin here promptly tomorrow morning at nine. Seating and parking will be limited and we ask that you arrive early. I also would like to remind you that it was Johnny's wish that in observance of the birth of Christ, the Prince of Peace, you light a candle on Christmas Eve and place the lighted candle in a prominent window of your home. Money for the candles was raised by members of the Young Peacemakers Club and parishioners from our church. The candles are being distributed in the vestibule. Please take a candle before you leave but limit yourselves to one candle per household. You are of course welcome to display as many candles of your own as you wish.

"Thank you again for coming today. Please wait for the ushers to escort you to the casket and family and exit the church through the center aisle."

An organist begins to play softly and the visitations begin. A few minutes after we pass out our first candles, two long-haired teenagers, a boy and a girl, come to join us at the table.

Maggie looks shocked. "I'm glad you came," she manages

to say.

"Why wouldn't we?" the girl answers, and then I realize who she is. It's Judis with James. "We didn't run him over if that's what you're thinking," Judis says. Luke and Mark look as if they're ready to stand up if they have to. James grabs two chairs and puts them at the table. No one says anything else to them and Maggie gives them candles to hand out.

Many people are still crying as they take the candles and say things like, "Thank you for doing this," and, "I wish he were here to help you," and, "He was such a fine young man. Keep up his work."

Dozens of kids are in line, too, and they look at me with a "Who are you?" look. When my parents finally make their way into the vestibule, I am surprised by who they are standing with. Officers Cole and Spencer look at me and Maggie and nod their heads. Officer Cole waves at James and Judis and gives them a little wink. I turn, shocked, to see if Maggie saw the wink, and turn toward my father again. He reads my confusion and gives me a "We'll talk later" look.

I steal peeks at Maggie, James, and Judis. They're busy handing out candles. After my parents have finally reached the casket, they talk to Johnny's parents for a couple of minutes and hug them before walking down the center aisle to us. My father signals me to come outside with him. I turn to Maggie to tell her

I'm stepping out for a minute and she says it's okay.

When we're away from the church, my father says, "There was quite a twist in the development of the case today. The results from the autopsy are in and they put it together with the testimony from several of the neighbors and a surprise key witness.

"A woman down the street apparently saw me pull out of our driveway and avoid getting hit by the car with one headlight. She said she saw me pass her house and then watched the other car approach Johnny's house and stop. With the snow and the dark she couldn't see very clearly, but she could tell they were stopped because of the bright brake lights. She also saw someone run from Johnny's house into the street toward the back of the car, but only after the car had already been stopped there for awhile. And then the figure disappeared. No car doors were opened and she never saw the figure ever actually approach the car. She said she then saw the car pull away. "

"That doesn't make sense," I say. "Does that mean they didn't hit him? Did another car come from behind them?"

"The woman says no."

"I don't understand," I say.   `

"Well, you aren't the only one who didn't understand," he says. "Remember he had approached the car from the rear. If Johnny had reached the side windows or somehow got to the front of the car, they would have seen him while the car was still

137

stopped; if he had reached the front of the car, they would never have been able to build enough momentum to hit him very hard. And remember, the neighbor said he'd 'disappeared'."

"So what happened?" I ask.

"The answer came with the autopsy," he said. "Johnny did die from a blow to his head, but it wasn't from a car. Evidently, when he ran out to meet the car, his feet slipped from under him at the curb because of the snow on the street and he landed directly on the back of his head. Because of the way he approached the car, the occupants in the car never even saw it happen. After waiting awhile, they assumed he wasn't coming and drove off with Johnny lying in the street behind them. The blow to his head had been so hard, it killed him almost instantly."

"So it never was a hit and run?"

"Apparently not," he says. "That seems like it's pretty much the scenario the police are going with. The autopsy backs it up completely. There's also another surprising piece of information."

"What?" I ask.

"Apparently, Johnny's younger brother was in the back seat of the car when it happened. His testimony as a key witness should verfy everything they believe happened."

Chapter 19

I stand staring at my father and my mother comes up behind us. "Are you okay?" she asks. "Did your father tell you what we found out?"

"Yes," I answer and turn to my father. "Do Frankie and his parents know what they suspect happened?"

"The only ones here who really know the outcome of the investigation are James and Judis. They were released from questioning less than an hour ago. Officers Cole and Spencer have been assigned to break the news to the Cannons. They're going to tell them after the wake to avoid upsetting them with all of these people here."

"But won't they be happy that he wasn't killed by a hit and run driver?"

"At this point, I think the only thing on their mind is that he's no longer alive. In any case, I think we should let the police be the ones who explain everything to them."

"Can I tell Maggie?" I ask.

"We promised Cole and Spencer we wouldn't share the information until Johnny's parents were informed. The only reason they told me was because I ended up involved in all of this. Maybe it's best you keep the information to yourself until his parents are told. Do you want us to wait here at the church for you until the wake is over to drive you home?"

"No," I say. "I think Maggie's planning to meet members of the Peacemakers Club at the pizza parlor for a while after this. I can walk from there."

My mother tells me to try not to get sauce on my suit because I'll need it clean for the funeral. I ask her if she can buy me black jeans, a black turtle neck shirt, and boots for tomorrow. She looks over at Maggie and the others and smiles, then she looks concerned. My father is staring too. I turn to see what they're looking at. A small group of teenagers are crowding the table and Maggie is in the middle of some sort of commotion. Luke and Mark are standing in front of James and Judis as if they're trying to keep them back from the other kids.

"I have to go," I say. "I'll see you at home."

"We're going to hang out here on the steps for a few minutes," he says. "Those kids might be the Disciples."

I walk over to the table and everyone stops talking. A tall kid in an expensive looking leather jacket is checking me over

140

and says, "Is this the new kid?" He reaches out his hand and I shake it.

"What's your name?" he asks.

"Peter," I answer.

"I'm Luther," he says. "You can call me Lou."

He looks me over again and says, "I see you're wearing their colors and hair style but that suit looks more like us. We're going over to the diner for a quick bite. Why don't you join us?"

"He can't. He's coming to the pizza parlor with us," Maggie says. "We're still not done giving out candles. In case you didn't notice, services are still going on for Johnny."

"I noticed," he says, and turns to me. "Can you talk for yourself or are you going to let a girl do the talking for you?"

"I'm going to let *this* girl do my talking for me," I say. I look at Maggie and she's smiling like crazy.

"I guess you *are* one of them," he says. Then he looks at James and Judis and says. "Are you coming?"

Maggie looks like she is about to answer but stops herself and lets them answer for themselves.

James answers for both of them. "We're staying to help, then we're going to the pizza parlor. We're with them too."

"Fine," Luther says. "You all deserve each other." Then he looks back at the kids he's with and spots Frankie coming towards us. "Hey, Frankie. Why don't you come with us to the diner?"

"Go to hell," Frankie says and turns to walk back to his parents.

Luther laughs and says, "Okay. Maybe I'll see you in hell." He motions to his friends and they follow him out of the church. Maggie looks surprised but steps back to let them pass.

We continue to give out the rest of the candles after the final prayers and see officers Cole and Spencer standing at the alter with Johnny's parents. They talk for a few minutes and Johnny's mother puts her hand to her mouth in shock. Both parents look at Frankie and he says something to them that makes his mother hug him. His expression is exactly the way its been: without a smile. They all start heading our way.

When they get to us, Johnny's mother is crying and just blurts it right out to Maggie. "It wasn't a hit and run," she says. "Johnny slipped on the ice and hit his head." She turns to James and Judis and says, "Frankie told us you were there to talk to Johnny and were going to tell him you wanted to start hanging around with him more and be a good influence on Frankie. He said you were going to tell him you still wanted to help with the candle vigil."

Maggie looks over at Judis and the two of them start to cry. Pretty soon everyone's crying. James, Maggie and Judis do a group hug thing and Maggie says, "I'm sorry I doubted both of you." All of this time Frankie has been standing there watching;

finally he walks up to Maggie and they have a hug and cry together.

When everyone stops hugging and crying, Johnny's father says, "A lot of people have brought food to the house for us and we want you all to come and eat with us. Johnny would have wanted you there and so do we." He reaches out and touches my shoulder and says, "Tell your parents that they're welcome, too. Apparently, there is enough food at the house for an army."

My parents are still standing in the doorway and I wave them to wait a minute. I start to tell them they're invited to the Cannon's but just as I'm telling them, Mr. Cannon comes over and invites them himself. My parents ask me if I need a ride and I ask Maggie. I tell her we can fit about five kids in the Escalade. "We have more than that," she says. "Let's all walk."

My mother overhears her and says, "Grab your coat from the car,"

"Let me guess," Maggie says. "It's a designer coat."

"Maybe," I say. And she laughs.

There are about eight of us on the church steps. Johnny's parents wave to us from the window of their car and remind us to come to the house for something to eat. Luther and Judis tell Maggie they'll meet us there because they have their car with them.

We start to walk and Luther pulls up to the curb. He looks

directly at me and shakes his head. A kid in the back seat holds up an L for loser and they all laugh as Luther pulls away.

"Ignore it," Maggie says. "Now you see why we don't want anything to do with them."

We work our way down the street to the pillared entrance of the Peninsula and I'm beginning to think I should have taken the ride with my parents. Nobody is talking very much and my ears are about to fall off from the cold. When we get to the house, I notice there are cars parked bumper to bumper in our driveway. My father evidently gave them permission to park there. I look down the street and a strange feeling passes through me as I watch people gather at the shrine in front of Johnny's house.

"Hey. Why did you stop walking?" Maggie says. "Aren't you coming in to Johnny's?"

"Not right now," I say. "I want to go into my house and warm up a minute before I go in there. I'll be there soon."

The rest of them say things like, "We'll see you inside" and walk on ahead of me, but Maggie holds back a minute, "Are you okay?" she asks.

"I'm feeling a little weird about going over there," I admit. I try to smile, and add, "Besides, my freaking ears are freezing. It's colder here than in the mountains."

She gives me a "poor baby" look and takes my hand for a moment. "Okay, but please come. I need you there and I know it's what Johnny would want us to do. I think his parents need company. My parents will probably be there too. I want you to meet them." I watch her catch up to the others and they all stop at the shrine. Maggie starts crying and Luke takes her hand to lead her into Johnny's front door.

When I get inside my own house my parents are getting ready to go next door.

"Are you going?" my mother asks.

"In a minute," I say. "I'm feeling kind of weird."

"You don't have to go if you don't want to," my father says. "We're going there out of respect but we feel a little strange going there too. Is Johnny trying to communicate with you?"

I look up at him quickly because I suddenly realize that is exactly what's happening. Johnny wants me to listen to something he is trying to say. A long shiver crawls up my backbone.

"Are you okay?" my mother asks.

"I think he's trying to tell me something," I say.

"Do you want us to stay here with you?" my father asks.

"I just need to warm up a few minutes first," I tell him. "I think he wants me there. You can go on ahead of me."

I close my door and know immediately what Johnny wants me to do. I reach for the framed photo sticking out from under my mattress, take it out, and stare into it.

"What are you trying to say to me?" I ask. I squeeze the

photo and yell at it. "What do you want?" Frustrated, I throw it toward my bed. But I miss. It bounces off the side of the mattress and crashes to the floor.

There at my feet is Johnny's answer. The glass and frame are completely broken and something is sticking out from the back of the photo. A sealed envelope. I bend to pick it up and my breath is sucked out of me. It's addressed to Frankie.

I pick it up slowly and place it on the bed then clean up the mess on my floor.

"Peter?" My mother knocks, opens my door, and sees the broken pieces still in my hand. Questions are written all over her face.

"It fell and broke when I tossed it to the bed." I set the pieces of glass and frame on my pillow and pick up the envelope. "This was behind the photo," I say. "It's addressed to his brother Frankie."

Chapter 20

I walk with my parents to Johnny's and can feel his eyes on me as we pass the shrine. When we get to the front door, his parents come rushing up to us.

"Thank you so much for coming," his mother says. My father hands her a cake he picked up at the bakery and she thanks him for it.

"I'm sorry for your loss," my mother says sadly, and they hug.

His mother tries not to cry and his father says, "Peter, thank you for helping with the candles. I appreciate your pitching in. Maggie and the kids are in the kitchen. Let me take you to them before I introduce your parents to some of the neighbors. Is that okay?" he asks. We nod yes and he leads me to Maggie. On the way, I look for Frankie to see if he's in with the adults, but there are too many people standing around.

"Here's Peter now," Maggie says when we get to the

kitchen.

His father pats my shoulder and rushes off to rejoin my parents.

"Are you okay?" Maggie asks.

"I'm okay," I say, and almost want to tell her what I found behind the picture, but there are too many kids with her. A lot of them say "hi" but I don't see Frankie. His letter is in my pocket and I'm not sure if this would be the time to give it to him if I did see him.

"There's plenty of food if you're hungry," Maggie says.

"I'm good," I say. James and Judis are by themselves in the corner, and it almost looks as if they're arguing about something.

"They've been in the corner talking since they got here," Maggie says. "I only talked with them for a second. They wanted to know if I saw Frankie."

"Did you?" I ask.

"No," she said. "He's probably with his relatives. I think he's having a hard time getting over what happened." And just as she says that, Frankie walks in. He goes directly to Judis and James and says something to them. James takes his arm but Frankie pulls it away and leaves through an outside door at the back of the kitchen.

"Something's up with them, "Maggie says. "Let's go over

and see if we can find out." She leads me over to them and asks Judis if everything's okay.

"It's fine," she says. "James and I have to leave. We're going to go out the back. If Johnny's parents ask about us just tell them we had to go." Before Maggie can answer, they turn and go out the same door Frankie used.

"Just let them go," Maggie says. "I think they're all feeling guilty about what happened. Can you blame them? Johnny would probably be alive right now if it wasn't for them."

I stare at her for a moment not knowing what to say and she says she has to go to the bathroom. Before I can answer her, she's gone. I walk to the window and look toward my house to see if Frankie, Judis, and James are out there. The light-sensors at the back of my house have been triggered and I see the three of them standing in plain sight arguing by our pool.

Nonchalantly, I walk so as not to be noticed and work my way to the back door. When no one's watching, I slip out into the yard. I'm still wearing my coat but the air is cold as I hurry out of reach of the light and behind a tree close enough to hear them.

"He would be alive if not for me," Frankie says.

"That's not true," Judis answers.

"It is," Frankie says. "And you're guilty too. I should have stopped hanging around with you like Johnny asked me to do. He knew this was going to happen and none of us listened. It

149

happened because of us. He begged us to stay away from Luther and the Disciples. He said something bad would happen. And it did."

"It was an accident," James says. "It was his time to die. That's the way it is."

"It's not the way it is," Frankie answers. "Luther is evil. My brother even said so. He tried to be friends with us to get to my brother. And he did. Luther needs to pay for what he did."

"You're just upset because of what happened to Johnny. Don't do anything stupid."

"I already did something stupid. It's time to do the right thing now. Luther has to pay for what he did to my brother." He turns to walk away and James grabs his arm. He pulls it free and heads right for the tree I'm standing behind. I stand perfectly still and pray that he doesn't see me. But he does. He stands staring into my face and then walks away quickly toward his house.

James and Judis don't follow him. They turn and walk toward the far side of my house and out of sight. By the time I turn toward Johnny's, Frankie's already in the house. I enter through the back door. Maggie is in the kitchen waiting for me.

"Where were you?" she asks.

"I saw Frankie go out and followed him. He was talking to Judis and James by our pool."

"Did you hear what they were talking about? Did they

know you were there?"

I take a quick look around the kitchen to see if Frankie is there, but he's not. Luke is pretty close and may be listening, so I say, "Do you want to go out for some fresh air?"

She looks at Luke and says, "Peter and I are going out for some fresh air if anybody asks for us." He gives her a nod and she heads for the door.

As we walk toward our pool and trigger the light-sensors, she says, "What did they say?"

"I think Frankie is blaming Luther and the Disciples for what happened to Johnny. He wants to go after him."

"That's stupid," Maggie says. "And dangerous."

"Do you think Luther will do something to him?"

"I think Luther will do what he's been trying to do all along. He'll get Frankie to listen to him long enough to get him over to his side. Luther hated Johnny for being so good, and the only way he could get to him was through Frankie. Now that Johnny isn't here to stop him, he's going to go after Frankie until he gets him to be as bad as he is."

I stare at her for a minute, then say, "Johnny is still here for Frankie." I pull the letter out of my pocket. "He left this letter behind the picture of the two of you. I broke the frame by accident and it was tucked in behind it."

"What does it say?"

151

"I didn't read it. It's marked 'Frankie'."

She takes it from me and stands there holding it in her hand. "Do you think we should---"

"No," I say. "I have to give it to him myself and let him open it. This is between Johnny and Frankie."

She frowns and agrees. "I think you should find him and give it to him before he does something stupid."

We walk toward the house and just as we get to the door, it swings open barely missing Maggie. Frankie is standing in the doorway.

"Stay away from me!" he shouts. "Both of you."

I start to answer him, but he turns back into the house. When we try to follow him in, he quickly disappears into one of the rooms. Mark and Paul are standing by the kitchen sink talking and Paul asks if everything is okay.

"Keep an eye out for Frankie," Maggie says. "Let me know if you see him go out. Stand by the back door."

Maggie doesn't say much more except, "I'm worried about what Frankie might do."

After about a half hour, people finally start leaving and my parents come into the kitchen to ask me if I'm ready to go. I look over at Maggie and she says she's leaving soon too. "Tomorrow is going to be a hard day because of the funeral," she says. "Will you stay with me during it? We're all meeting at the funeral parlor at eight tomorrow morning."

My mind flashes to what my father said in his emails about hearing voices of the dead in the cemetery. A tingling crawls up my spine.

"Will you stay with me?" she asks again.

"Sure," I say.

My parents are wearing their coats and Johnny's parents hug them and thank them for coming. They tell me I'm welcome there anytime. Frankie could use a friend right now. "Will you all be coming to the funeral? I appreciate your being here with us today, but if you have something else to do---"

"No, no. Of course we'll be there," my father says. They hug again and Johnny's father says, "The back door will probably be easier for you. I don't think there's much snow on the ground."

I wave good-bye to the kids in the kitchen and Maggie gives me an uncomfortable hug as my parents watch. Her parents are watching too and say it's nice to have met me.

The light-sensors go on as we reach the pool and my father says, "Looks like someone's been out here. There are footprints all over the yard."

I don't answer. I go into the house and directly to my room to plop myself on my bed. It's eight forty-five. I'm exhausted but I feel as if I'm being pulled away. I get up and open my bedroom door slowly. My parents' door is shut. Quickly and quietly I walk to the mantel of the fireplace. There on its side is my grandfather's book of diary poems. A pink ribbon is marking a page. I open to it.

That life
Is a series of tests,
A constant battle
Between right and wrong,
Is certain.
The uncertainty
Lies in our strength
To endure both
The consequences of our decisions
And our fate.

Chapter 21

I roll his words over and over again in my mind. "That life is a series of tests, a constant battle between right and wrong is certain. The uncertainty lies in our strength to endure both the consequences of our decisions and our fate."

My eyes are heavy. I shut off the lamp at the side of my bed and pull one pillow up against me as I usually do, hug it close, and bury the side of my face in the other pillow.

My grandfather stands there smiling at me. I walk over to him.

"It's you," I say.

"Yes, it is," he answers.

He looks just as he did before, wearing a polo shirt and slacks and looking comfortable and sure of himself. "Do you think your friend is ready to face his decisions and his fate?" he asks.

"Do you mean Johnny?" I ask. "Is my mission to help him to cross over?"

He laughs. "Is that what you believe your mission is? Do

you believe an Earth-Bound's only mission is to save those who have already left their life on earth?"

"Isn't it?" I ask.

"No," he says. "You must also try to help those still with you. Help them from getting into the place of lost souls in the first place. It's the mission of all living things to help one another."

I look at him confused and then realize what he must be saying. "Do you mean Frankie? Is my mission to save Frankie?"

"Your mission is to save as many lost souls as you can."

"But is my **immediate** *mission to help Johnny save Frankie? Is Frankie in danger?"*

I look around the room for him to answer me, but he's gone. He isn't standing in front of me anymore. I am in bed and his body is on my bed with its back to me. I squeeze him and shake him to make him answer, and then push him off the bed.

When I realize I've been dreaming, I sit up in a sweat and see my pillow on the floor. It's dark in my room but light is streaming in from my glass sliding doors. The outside light-sensors have been triggered. I rush to my feet to see who or what is out there. It's snowing hard and I have to adjust my eyes to make out a figure as it moves its way through our yard and out toward our neighbors' back yard opposite Johnny's house.

Someone is by the shore at the edge of the lake. Frankie?

I quickly struggle into some clothes, pull on a coat, and go out to follow him. By the time I get to the shore he's gone, but his footprints are easy to track. They lead up to the right of our neighbor's house and out onto Dexter Lane. From the center of the street, I try to get my bearings. In the streetlight up by Johnny's shrine, I can see the snowflakes coming down heavily and slow, but the footprints go in the opposite direction toward the pillars and pizza parlor. My neighbor, a couple of houses away from ours, is watching from behind her curtained window. She ducks out of the way when she knows I've seen her. I turn away and continue after Frankie.

The tracks lead to the stone pillars and stop. I've lost him. There are no footprints to my right or left and none going toward the pizza parlor across the street. The owner is busy behind the counter and no customers are in there with him.

"I told you to leave me alone and to stop following me," a voice says from behind me, scaring me nearly out of my pants. "I turn quickly to see Frankie standing by the far side of the pillar. He's carrying a paper bag clutched close to his belly.

"I have something to give you," I say. "It's from your brother Johnny."

"That's bullshit," he answers. "Johnny's dead and you didn't even know him."

I search into my pocket for the letter and try handing it to him. He doesn't reach for it. "Take it," I say. "Your name is on it. I found it behind the framed picture of Johnny and Maggie."

"How did you get the picture?" he asks.

"I was looking at it at the shrine in front of your house and someone came out and scared me. I ran with it and kept it in my room. It fell and broke and this was behind it."

He looks down at it, shifts the paper bag to his left hand, and grabs the letter with his right. We stand there looking at each other for a moment getting covered in falling snow. Finally he begins walking to the pizza parlor without saying anything. I follow behind and he doesn't object.

Inside, the smell is wonderful and the warmth sends shivers through me.

"What are you guys doing out tonight? I thought I was going to be the only one in here, hey," the pizza man says suddenly, "Frankie, I'm sorry about Johnny. I couldn't come to the wake because I had no one to cover me. Did your mother get the pizzas I sent over for her? I'll be at the funeral tomorrow. Let me make you a pizza on me."

Frankie doesn't acknowledge him. He sits there with the snow melting off his hair and stares at the letter. "How do I know you didn't write this yourself?" he asks.

"I didn't," I say.

158

He doesn't ask any more questions. The bag gets tucked securely between his legs and he rips the letter open right there in front of me. My heart is pounding and I can barely breathe, so when a hand touches my shoulder, I jump to my feet and scream. The pizza man screams too and Frankie jumps up screaming with us. The paper bag falls to the floor and a small hand gun falls out.

Chapter 22

The pizza man and I stand staring at the gun before the man dives
on it and picks it up. "What are you doing with this, Frankie?
Why are you carrying this with you?"

"Give it to me," Frankie says. "It's none of your business
why I want it."

"I've known you and your brother since you were born.
My heart is broken over what happened to Johnny. Of course it's
my business."

"Give it back," Frankie demands.

"I'll give it to your father. I have a permit to carry a gun
because of the store, and I'll keep it with my gun until he comes
for it. Why do you have this, Frankie?"

"I told you it's none of your business," he shouts. He holds
out his hand but the man turns his back to him and returns to the
counter. "Fine," Frankie shouts. "Keep the damn gun. I can get
another one." He goes for the door. I follow him out, but he turns

on me in the parking lot. "Why are you following me? I told you to stay the hell away from me."

"Read the letter," I say, and I pray that it says something that will calm him down enough for me to talk some sense into him.

"You want me to read the damned letter?" he shouts. "Fine. I'll read the damned letter." He walks over to the light of the large window and reads out loud from the letter still in his hand.

Dear Frankie,

If you are reading this I'm already gone. My dying wasn't about you. I knew something was going to happen to me. I knew for awhile now. Sometimes things have to happen. It's called fixed destiny. But some things aren't fixed. If we make the right decisions we can stop bad things from happening and change our destiny. You have time to do the right things, Frankie. Please, think before you act. I won't be there to force you. Right decisions have to be your own decisions. You don't have to do it alone. Pick the right people to help you think right. Avoid being tempted by the wrong people and don't blame them for what they do. Just don't do it with them or let them take you down. I love you so much Frankie. I want to be with you together in the Light someday. Please do what you have to do to get here when it's really your time. Please Frankie.

Love, Johnny.

He's crying like crazy now and I don't know what to do. I move in closer to him and he puts his arms around me and starts crying real loud in my ear with his wet face pressed close to mine. "I miss him so much. He died because of me," he says.

I move my face away from his a little and my voice comes out almost in a whisper. "He didn't die because of you. He died because of his fate. He told you that in the letter. But you *will* hurt him if you do anything stupid. If you really love him you'll do the right thing."

I let him go because it feels awkward hugging him on the

street in front of the bright window. He looks directly into my eyes still crying and he can see that I've been crying too. "I know I can never replace your brother," I say. "But we're neighbors now. I live right next door. I never had a big brother or best friend and I'm going to need a friend going to a new school and all. Let's both show Luther and the Disciples the right way to do things."

"You should have offered to help when I came to your doors and called out your name."

"I didn't know who it was. I thought it was Johnny trying to talk to me. Do you forgive me?"

He wipes away his snot with his sleeve and says. "I guess so. I need to go inside and talk to Tony about the gun so I don't get into big trouble with my father. I also need to eat because I didn't eat at the house tonight. I'm starving. Do you want to come in and share the free pizza Tony promised me?"

"Definitely," I say. "I'll help you talk to Tony, too. You're already making good decisions. Especially since you decided to share the pizza." I give him a big smile. "I didn't eat at your house either. I love the pizza in this place."

He makes a kind of snorty laugh, wipes his eyes and snot with his sleeve again, and smiles back at me. I put my hand on his shoulder in a big brother kind of way and we go inside the pizza parlor to eat together.

When Tony sees us come in, he says to Frankie, "Where

are they?"

"Where are what?" Frankie asks.

"The bullets. There aren't any in the gun or the bag."

"My father doesn't keep the bullets with his guns," Frankie tells him.

Tony and I look at each other and then we both look at Frankie. "What were you going to do with this gun? I thought you were you going to hurt yourself with it."

"No," he says. "I was going to teach someone a lesson."

"Are you crazy?" Tony asks. "Who were you going after with this gun? How do you know that he or she didn't have a gun with bullets? Don't you know you could have been killed with an unloaded gun?"

"I was only going to scare the crap out of Luther and tell him to stay away from me."

Tony looks at him sadly and says, "You could have gotten yourself killed. Do you know what that would have done to your parents? Especially now with Johnny gone."

"I wasn't thinking about that," Frankie says. "A lot's been going on lately. Don't you think?"

Tony frowns at him and says, "Do you guys still want that pizza?"

"Definitely," we both answer at the exact same time and give each other a high-five.

"Listen," Frankie says to Tony, "My father will kill me if he knows I took his gun. I need to slip it back where it was before he finds out. I'm okay now. I swear. And it doesn't even have any bullets. You can trust me. How long did you say you knew me? All my life right?"

I glance at Tony. "It's okay." I say. "I'll be sure he puts it back. He's really okay now."

Tony looks doubtful, but he says, "Let me think about it until you're done with the pizza."

After the last bite we sit there for a few minutes and Tony comes over to the table with the paper bag. "I'll give it to Peter to carry for you. But I'm only doing it because it doesn't have bullets. I think you're smart enough to put it back where you got it. I hope I'm not making a mistake trusting you."

"I can be trusted," Frankie says. I take the bag and tuck it under my arm then thank Tony for the pizza. Frankie thanks him too. We go across the street to the pillars and start working our way up Dexter Lane. The snow has stopped. A quarter of the way up the block we hear a car slow down just behind us. Frankie stops walking and I clutch the bag with the gun in my hand before grabbing his arm quickly, then turn to see who's pulling up at the curb beside us.

"What are you guys doing out here? I've been looking for you."

I take a real deep breath of relief and walk to the passenger side widow. "We just went for pizza," I tell my father, "This is Frankie. Remember? Johnny's brother."

"Well, I'm glad to see you together, but you had us worried. Get in. I'll give you a lift home."

"We're almost there now," Frankie says. "I still have something I want to say to Peter."

"Alright," my father says. "But don't stay out too long. It's cold and slippery out here and you have a long day ahead of you tomorrow. Both of you."

His tires spin on ice as he drives away from us and we walk together to Johnny's shrine. On the way, Frankie says, "Thanks for tonight. You don't have to worry about starting the new school. I'll be there for you and so will Maggie and the rest of the gang. I'm going to tell Maggie that I want to take charge of the candle vigil on Christmas Eve. Johnny would have wanted me to."

"That's another real good decision," I say. "A real good decision."

When we get to the shrine, Frankie stops and stares at a place where Johnny may have slipped. I'm covered in goose bumps and a tingling begins. It feels like my skin is on fire. An eight-by-ten photo of Johnny has been stapled to the tree and there's a candle flickering under it. It flickers real fast for a couple of seconds and then goes out. Just as I'm about to say something, it lights back up again, only bigger and brighter than it was before. Johnny's face is easier to see now, and he's staring back at the two of us with his brother Frankie's Mona Lisa smile.

"Here," I say, and hand him the paper bag. "Swear you'll put it back where you found it and will never take it out again."

"I swear," he says.

Chapter 23

I wake up with a start and shelter my eyes from the light streaming through the glass sliding doors. This time it's daylight. Did I sleep through the whole night? Did I dream? I rack my brain to remember any details. Why didn't Johnny or my grandfather come to me?

It's minutes before seven am. Maggie expects me to be at the funeral parlor by eight. As quickly as possible, I jump from the bed and run into the kitchen. "Hey," my father says. "I was just about to come in for you. We have to be at the funeral parlor in less than an hour."

"Why didn't you wake me?" I ask.

"You were sleeping so soundly, I figured you needed your rest. Are you okay? You didn't talk much when you got home. I wondered how things went with Frankie. I was surprised to see you with him last night. I didn't think you really knew each other."

"It's a long story," I say. "I'll fill you in on the way to the funeral parlor. Maggie's expecting me at eight. I was hoping that if I got to sleep early I would dream about Grandpa or Johnny and get an idea of what to expect today."

"Did you dream about them?"

"I don't remember dreaming of anything," I say. "Will I hear the voices of the dead? Will they try to talk to me at the cemetery?"

"I don't know," he answers. "I'm a little worried about that myself. But they aren't going to harm you. They're just looking for answers. Some of them don't even know they're dead."

My mother comes into the kitchen already dressed. "You'd better get a move on if you want to be on time. I set the clothes out you asked me to get for you. They're pretty close to what your friends were wearing at the wake yesterday. Are you going to take a shower?"

"I'll take a quick one but I don't have much time," I say, "thanks for getting the clothes."

I rush into the bathroom, take a quick shower and hurry to my room to get my new black turtleneck shirt, black pants and black boots. I get dressed, run to the bathroom to comb my hair, brush my teeth, and pop a zit, all in about two minutes.

"That was quick," my mother says when she sees me "Do you want a little something to eat? These things can last quite awhile."

"I'm not hungry," I tell her. "I ate pizza with Frankie pretty late last night."

"Your father told me," she says. "I can't wait to hear how that happened. You never even mentioned him when we got home last night. I thought you were in your room sleeping."

My father comes in from the outside and says the car's warmed up. We hurry out the door and I tell them everything that happened as we drive along – only I leave out the part about the gun.

Just before we get to the funeral parlor, I say, "I 'm pretty sure now that keeping Frankie out of trouble is what Johnny needed me for."

"Sounds about right," my father says, "I'm sure he can use a friend right now." He pulls to the curb and looks out at a crowd of people. "We're here."

The funeral parlor is an old white village mansion with huge pillars and a covered entrance-way. Two men in black suits are in the parking lot directing traffic. My father stops at the main doors and a third man helps us get out, takes the keys, and drives our car away. Maggie and several boys are waiting inside at the top of the stairs. Maggie, Luke and Mark stand staring like they're shocked at the sight of me. All of the boys are wearing suits. Maggie's wearing an expensive looking black dress that looks amazing on her.

"Why are you dressed like that?" she asks.

"I thought this was what I was supposed to wear," I say.

"It was—yesterday," she says. "Today's the funeral. You were supposed to wear a suit."

I groan pretty loud and my parents are trying not to smile. Maggie bursts out laughing.

I turn to my mother and give her a look, but she says, "We don't go to many funerals. When you said those were the clothes you had to wear, I took your word for it."

"You look fine," Maggie says. "No one cares what you're wearing as long as you're here."

The funeral parlor suffocates me with its smell of flowers everywhere. A tall man in a black suit asks my father if he will be driving in the procession. "I'm not sure," my father answers. "I'm fortunately new at this. Is there going to be a procession?"

The man tells him that after the final prayer by the priest, the family will go up to the casket to say their final prayers. At that time, everyone else will go out to form a procession of cars behind the hearse and family limousine. "One of our funeral directors will be lining up the cars. We'll first follow the hearse to the church and after the services, to the cemetery." My father turns a little white. The man thinks it's because my father is nervous about making mistakes. He says, "You'll do fine. Keep

171

your headlights and emergency flashers on. You shouldn't have any problems. I'll put you somewhere in the middle of the line. We have almost seventy cars in the procession. Just follow the car in front of you. Half of Starlight Village will be in the line. You'll be fine."

The man motions for us to go into another room to get into a short line of people waiting to go up to the casket. Maggie takes my arm and leads us into the room filled with crying people sitting in chairs, all facing the open casket with Johnny's dead body in it.

"I thought the wake was yesterday at the church," I say.

"It was," she answers. "This is just so his family and friends can see him one last time before they take him to the cemetery. Only special people are allowed here today."

The line goes quickly and my parents kneel by the body. I try to look at their faces to see if Johnny is talking to them, but their backs are to me. They make the sign of the cross and turn around, but look pretty normal. When they go over to hug Johnny's parents, I see Frankie staring at Johnny. With my parents out of my way, my view of Johnny's face is perfectly clear – and his voice is even clearer.

"Don't be frightened," I hear the voice say.

My heart nearly stops beating and I search his lips half expecting them to be moving.

172

"I know you talked to Frankie last night. If you hadn't been there his whole fate would have changed and he would have been killed. Luther would have called the police and they would have killed Frankie when they saw him with a gun. It was the reason you were brought to Starlight. Frankie has missions he needs to complete just as you do. He would never have been able to do them without your help. Your grandfather said to tell you he's proud of you and that you shouldn't worry about the cemetery. You and your parents won't be hearing voices there. He also said to tell your father he will always be there for you if you need him."

I'm nearly breathless and turn to my parents who are waiting by the chairs watching me. They know what must be happening.

I turn back to the lifeless body and the voice begins again. *"You are a credit to all Earth-Bounds. I wish I could be there with you. There is so much work left for you to do. So many souls to save. You won't be hearing from me again. Your grandfather will be escorting me to the Light today. Take care of Frankie for me. Tell him I love him."*

Suddenly, there is a hand on my shoulder and I jump up from the kneeler.

"I didn't mean to scare you," Maggie says. "But you aren't supposed to say a whole mass for him here." I turn to face her and

173

she says, "God, you look like you're going to faint. Are you okay?"

I stare at her as I try to catch my breath. She panics and calls my father over. "He looks pretty pale," she says.

My father takes one arm, and Frankie comes over and takes the other. I'm totally embarrassed and when I try to talk, nothing comes out. I try again but my mouth won't move. Johnny's parents run to us and I finally can hear myself say, "I'm okay." They all look at me like they don't believe me, and I say it again, "I'm okay. Really."

They give me room and I begin breathing normally, until Frankie takes my arm again. "I'll bring him out for fresh air," he says.

My father says he'll come too, but Maggie takes my other arm. They walk me past dozens of people in the chairs who are staring and shaking their heads in sympathy. Out in the foyer one of the men in a black suit offers me a paper cup with water. I drink it and thank him.

"We have a lounge here in the back," he says. "Why don't you go in with your friends and rest a minute."

In the room there are a couple of Johnny's young cousins, but their parents poke their heads in and tell them to leave to give us privacy. Frankie helps me to the sofa as Maggie goes for more water, then he stares at me with a weird look on his face before he says, "Are you like him? Can you hear dead people? I think I heard him talking to you."

"What did you say?" I ask.

"I think I heard him talking to you," he repeats.

And then something occurs to me. "How old are you?" I ask.

"I just turned fourteen last month. Why?"

Chills run through me. Frankie is the same age my grandfather, mother, father and I started realizing we were Earth-Bounds.

"Why?" Frankie asks.

"We'll talk about it later," I tell him and he nods an okay..

My father pops his head in to see if I'm alright and says they're going to do the final prayer.

"We need to go to the car, but if you can't---"

"I'm fine," I say.

Frankie is about twenty cars ahead of us in the family limousine and Maggie is about ten cars ahead with her parents. I'm sitting in the front seat with my father; my mother is in the back. As we move along slowly my father says, "Are you sure you're okay? Did he talk to you?"

"Yes," I say. "He told me that the reason I was brought here was to change Frankie's fate." I pause and add, "I saved Frankie from being killed last night."

175

My mother practically jumps up from her seat. "What do you mean you saved him from being killed? What happened with you and Frankie last night? What aren't you telling us?"

"It was nothing," I say. "Frankie had his father's gun---"

Both of them shout at once, "What?"

"It didn't have bullets in it and he never even got to use it. He was going to go after Luther, the leader of the Disciples and accuse him of causing Johnny's death, but I followed him and we went for pizza instead. "

My mother gives me her "What are you not telling me?" look.

"That's all it was," I say. "Johnny said if I hadn't stopped him Frankie would have gone to Luther's and the police would have killed him there thinking he was some kind of killer. Maybe I'm like his guardian angel or something."

My father smiles sadly. "Nope. His *Earth-Bound Angel.* Did Johnny say anything else to you?"

"Yeah," I say. "He said my grandfather's proud of me and we shouldn't worry about any of the dead talking to us at the cemetery. He said Grandpa took care of that and he's taking him into the Light today. He also said to tell you that he will always be there for me if I need him."

My father fights to keep himself from crying as he reaches out to take my hand. "We're all proud of you," he says. My

176

mother is starting to cry too and she puts her hand on my shoulder.

"He also said I'm a credit to all Earth-Bounds and he wishes he could be here with me. He said there is still a lot more work to do. Many more souls to save."

"He's right about that," my father says. "And your mother and I will be here if you need us, too. As long as we can." He stops talking and looks at my mother through the rear-view mirror. His tears are rolling down his cheeks now. "If something unexpected should happen---."

"Don't," my mother says. "We'll be fine. If anything should happen, Peter will go on and do whatever he was meant to do, just the way you did when fate took *your* father."

My stomach turns and I see that my father is hiding his face from me.

"Is something going to happen to you?" I ask. "*Tell me*," I shout. "I want to know."

He looks at my mother again through the rear view mirror and wipes his eyes with the back of his sleeve. "It's just a premonition," he says. "Everything will be fine."

Chapter 24

"I want to know what the premonition is," I demand.

"We've alluded to this before," she says. "Your father believes that since his father died on his seventeenth birthday, he will die on yours."

My stomach drops. My birthday is on Christmas Day. My father avoids looking at me.

"Look at me," I say. "Are you just *afraid* of what will happen? Do you know for sure? Did you dream about it?"

He's still looking away, and my mother has turned away too. "Is something going to happen to both of you? I need to know!" I shout.

"Listen. It doesn't have to happen just because you dreamed it. In the letter Johnny wrote to Frankie he said something that makes sense to me now. He said sometimes things have to happen. It's called fixed destiny. But some things aren't fixed. If we make the right decisions we can stop bad things from happening. He told Frankie that he had time to do the right thing. And when Frankie did do the right thing and didn't go to Luther's, he didn't get killed. There's time to change what can happen. If it worked for Frankie, it can work for you. I need to know your premonition so I can help you change it."

My mother and father look at each other incredulously. "He has a point," my mother says. "If it worked for Frankie, it could work for us."

My father wipes away tears with his sleeve again and asks my mother, "What have we created?"

My mother gives him a half-smile and says, "A pure Earth-Bound. An amazingly wonderful pure Earth-Bound."

Our conversation ends there because we are at the church. A suited-man walks along the line of cars pointing us into the parking lot where my father pulls into a space. We follow the crowd to the church steps, past the hearse with Johnny's casket on the tailgate, where two lines of West Point cadets in uniform turn to face each other as a path for the pall-bearers who will take Johnny's casket up the steps to the church doors.

Maggie is in the side aisle near the alter as we enter and waves us into the seats she's reserved for us behind the family pew. When we are settled in, Maggie takes my hand and organ music begins to play. Heads turn and six men carrying Johnny, three on each side, enter the church and set the casket on a carrier with wheels. The priest is at the alter with two altar servers, boys, at his sides each carrying a lighted candle. A third alter server, a girl, carries a folded cloth, and a fourth server carries a golden chalice with some sort of wand and holy water. I recognize the four servers as members of Johnny's Young Peacemaker's Club.

The priest says a prayer, and a new hymn begins as he and the alter servers march down to the casket, sprinkle it with holy water, and turn around to face the alter to lead the procession past the congregation. Behind the casket are Johnny's parents and family. Crying. As they pass us, Frankie glances quickly in my direction and then at the ceiling of the church. I look up to see what he is staring at and my body is no longer with me.

I am in another world far from the church. The organ music is in the distance somewhere carrying me through a lazy river of music and space. But there are no real people. Only thoughts and memories. Everything I have ever seen or known or heard about is there for me. As if every thought I have ever had is occurring at the exact same time. I am being born and crying with my mother, and running through the woods at the house in the Catskills and back to the hospital at my birth again. Cave men appear when I think of them, and astronauts float through space in full gear. My life and everyone's life before me is there for me to experience or re-experience, second by second, to live again and again or be a part of as much as I wish. Dreamlike yet

real. Johnny and my grandfather are there somehow, but not as
they were. It is all different from anything I have ever known:
unimaginably peaceful, painless, fearless, guiltless and
comforting. I sense, but I have no ears, nose, eyes, or brain. A
weightless mass of energy and soul – and the sensation is
heavenly.

And then, I am drawn away by Frankie's voice at the
podium. The silence is deafening as he lowers his eyes to the
book he is holding and continues reading from the Book of
Ecclesiastes.

There is an appointed time for everything,
and a time for every affair under the heavens.
A time to give birth, and a time to die;
a time to plant, and a time to uproot the plant.
A time to kill, and a time to heal;
a time to tear down, and a time to build.
A time to weep, and a time to laugh;
a time to mourn, and a time to dance.

a time to be silent, and a time to speak.
A time to love, and a time to hate;
a time of war, and a time of peace.

He lifts his head and looks out at the crowded church, and
then at me. "My brother Johnny seemed to know the time for
everything. He knew when to be quiet or scream, when to laugh

and when to cry. I hated it sometimes because he was so perfect. But no matter how jealous I got or hated the things he did, I never hated *him*. Nobody did. Everybody loved Johnny. He saw things about life that most people can't see." All heads bob yes in agreement. "He even knew enough to stay away from me when I was angry or stubborn or acting like a jerk. " Several people laugh quietly. "He helped me to find peace when I thought I needed war. Nobody loved peace as much as my brother. I know he's found it now." He starts to cry but pulls himself together.

"On Christmas Eve Johnny hoped he could see lighted candles in every house in Starlight Village as a symbol of world peace. I want to make sure he gets his wish. I hope you do, too." He looks up out into the church and says, "Will he get his wish?" The church breaks out into a muffled roar with people shouting "Yes!" and applauding.

Quietly, he raises his hand to bring his audience under his command much the way I'm sure his brother was able to do. "My brother used to say that life and peace are worth fighting for. It's what we all must do. We can never give up."

The congregation applauds again and Frankie steps from the podium where his mother stands waiting to speak. She hugs him and kisses his cheek and takes her place at the microphone as silence fills the church again.

She clears her throat and fights to keep her composure. "I

don't know what to say about Johnny that you don't already know. I have never known anyone quite like him. I listened to the lines of the Ecclesiastes that Frankie read to you and I know that there is truly an appointed time for everything. Johnny would not want me to mourn for him. I believe Frankie is right about Johnny's finding his eternal peace. But I find it hard right now to believe that his father and I won't be mourning his loss for the rest of our lives. I am not sure I can bear not seeing or hearing him every day, or not holding him after all of these years of loving him so much. In the few short years he's been alive, he's experienced more than some people live in a lifetime. He has inspired and impacted the lives of so many in his speeches and through his actions. The number of people in this church today is a testimony of Johnny's ability to affect others." She turns and points to the priest who has been sitting at the alter listening and says, "Father joked with me earlier about putting up a picture of Johnny in the vestibule later because no one could fill a church the way Johnny could. His picture would remind all of us that he will always be here watching us." People laugh nervously then start crying again.

"When I asked Johnny one time if there was anything he would wish for if he had three wishes, he said he would wish for: peace in the world; eternal happiness for everyone he loved; and a chance to ride a dragon."

With the words barely out of her mouth, I swear I can see

him up there riding that dragon and laughing, and I imagine my grandfather waiting in line for his chance to ride it with him.

The mass ends shortly after his mother's speech and the pallbearers and priest form another procession to take Johnny down the aisle one last time. I don't watch as the casket passes me because I know the real Johnny isn't in there. I look up instead at the light coming from the stained glass windows.

When the casket reaches the back of the church, the priest blesses it one last time and walks to the front of it to lead the pallbearers down the steps and through the line of the West Pointers. As the casket passes, each cadet salutes in turn.

I watch as they put the casket in the hearse and my father touches my shoulder before whisking me off to our car where we join the motorcade to the cemetery. Once we arrive, we pull into the gates and my father takes a deep breath, but nothing seems to happen. My grandfather has kept his promise and the graves are silent. The suited man points to where we're to park ,and after a long wait, we are escorted to the crowd of people who have surrounded a freshly dug grave with Johnny's casket suspended by belts above it. Maggie comes over and takes my arm and the priest begins praying. I focus on Maggie and finally hear him say, "To everything there is a season, and a time to every purpose under heaven, a time to be born and a time to die."

On Christmas Eve no house was without at least one lit candle. Frankie saw to that and made sure that we all helped to make it happen. At midnight, practically the whole town, including Luther and his followers, were at the church to celebrate peace, the birth of Christ, and the memory of Johnny Cannon.

According to my father's premonition, my parents were scheduled to die in a car accident on the way back from the church at approximately twelve forty-five. Forty-five minutes into my birthday. It never happened, of course, because I made them walk home from the church with me and Maggie.

"Are you coming in?" my father asked when we finally arrived home. "Maggie's parents are coming to get her since you won't let me drive."

I smiled and said. "We'll wait for them out here. We're going next door for a few minutes," I said.

We walked over arm and arm, and I'm sure Johnny was up there smiling when we lit a candle at the shrine, and when I kissed Maggie near the flowers by the roadside.

When I got home, I went directly to my room, and there on my bed was a paperback book, ready to be published: *EMAILS TO A PARANOMAL: The Diary Poems of Damien Darrk,* with a note from my father on a page marked off by a pink ribbon.

There are a lot of details in these poems that were not in the emails you've read. I hope you'll enjoy reading them. Your mother and I could not be any prouder of you. May the spirits be with you.

Love, Dad

I smiled to myself and jumped up on my bed to begin reading.

V.T. DACQUINO

EMAILS
TO A
PARANORMAL

THE DIARY POEMS OF
DAMIEN DARRK

EMAILS
TO
A PARANORMAL

THE DIARY POEMS OF
Damien Darrk

V.T. Dacquino

A VTD EduCon Book

Published by

VTD EduCon Books

Mahopac, NY 10541

For further information go to:

www.vtdacquino.com

ISBN:0-9904814-0-9

EAN-13:978-0-9904814-0-9

To:

June, Jamie, Vinny,

Christian and Cadence

Special thanks to Jeff Edrich and Steve Haggerty for their help with formatting the manuscript and to the Mahopac Library Writers Group for helping to keep literacy alive in Mahopac --and in me.

Table of Contents

CHAPTER I

My Name

Part 1
I

I know you may find my name

To be strange

And may think that no caring parent

Would name a child

Damien Darrk.

The truth is

I've created this name to protect my identity

And will tell you my real name

Only when I know

You can be trusted.

II

I am being visited

By a spirit.

I suspect she is a young girl

On a mission.

The reason she has chosen my room

And me,

A seventeen year old boy,

May be connected to why

My father was killed

And why I am coming to you.

III

She'll come again tonight
After midnight
When the house is quiet,
Whispering behind my closet door,
Moaning
As she's done for months.
I'm not afraid.
I know I must help her
But I am helpless
Without you.

IV

I've chosen you
To receive these diary poems
Because of your ability to communicate
With spirits.
I believe
As you do
That there are no coincidences
When it comes to matters of the supernatural.
I also believe as you do
That dead people live here.

V

She came to me
Several months ago,
On Oct 30,
The night of my birthday.
My mother threw a surprise party.
When it was over
I went to my room
Where something called to me
From my closet,
Moaning.

VI

I wasn't sure what I was hearing.
I laughed to myself
Thinking I was being pranked.
"Come out," I said,
"I know you geeks are in there."
But no one answered.
The moaning continued.
I pulled the covers off
And walked to the door at the foot of my bed.
The moaning got louder.

VII

I felt coldness
Coming from the closet,
But not like any coldness I've ever felt.
It seeped through my skin
And entered me from every pore.
I reached for the doorknob
Wishing to end the silly prank,
But the knob was already turning.
The door opened
To an almost empty room.

VIII

My clothes hung from hangers
Like ghosts,
Unmoving,
The shelf above them motionless.
From somewhere on the floor
In the corner of the darkness,
The moaning
Became a whimper,
Like a puppy without a mother
Crying for help.

IX

I dropped to my knees
And listened as the whining
Took on a strange rhythm,
Song like,
Childlike,
A lullaby that mothers use
To quiet their children.
Then there was silence,
Until I heard
My own mother's voice behind me.

X

I gave her a poor excuse
For kneeling by my closet
At midnight
And have given her a dozen more excuses
For my strange behaviors.
She doesn't understand any of this
So I'm turning to you
To shed some light
On the mystery that is haunting my room
And me.

Part 2

I

Somehow,

I managed to sleep the night of my birthday

And spent most of the next day, Halloween,

At my computer web-searching your name.

Halloween is not my favorite holiday.

My father died last year

On Halloween night

Returning from a three day business trip

Rushing to get home

To my mother and me.

II

When the police arrived

To tell us about the accident

We thought they were trick-or-treaters,

Until we answered the door and saw their faces.

I stood there

By my mother

With candy to give them

But they were only there

To give us

Their condolences.

III

My father
Was a very good father.
He gave me everything
I needed.
Even what I didn't.
My memories of him
Will live with me forever.
I am grateful for the time we spent together,
But I need your help
To contact him.

IV

My mother
Is lonely.
She wanders around our house
Like he will suddenly appear as he was,
To hold her
As he used to.
But we both know
Good husbands
And good fathers
Don't live in this world forever.

V

I imagine
That you
In your line of work as a paranormal
Have communicated with ghosts
Like my father,
Or the girl in my closet
Who may have been taken suddenly
Without a chance
To say
Good-bye.

VI

Do you see them
And hear them
Out there
Floating in some weird haze,
Moaning in closets
Or hovering frantically
Over the cars they've been killed in,
Still trying to drive home
To families
They'll never reach.

VII

How closely do I have to listen
To hear their whispers in the wind,
Or separate the ticking of the clock
From the tapping of their fingers
On my brain?
Or recognize that I must be dreaming
When the girl from the closet
Floats close enough
To brush my cheeks
With hers.

VIII

Have you ever lost people you loved?
Do you feel them
When you lie awake in the night?
Do they talk to you in words
Or come in cold rushes through you?
Do they pull across your skin
Like a ballerina's tights
Hugging closely to you
Making it impossible
For you to breathe?

IX

Do dead people die,
Or do they linger here
In some kind of temporary prison?
Can I see them if I try?
Can they see me?
How dead Is dead?
I know who you are;
I've seen you on the computer.
Do you say what you believe
And believe the things you say?

X

These poems should have arrived to you by now
Please read them.
I need you to come to her.
Does she speak for herself
Or my father?
Can you tell me what she wants from me?
Please don't be afraid.
I am different from most kids my age but not insane.
If you believe in what you say,
Please believe in me.

Part 3

I

I haven't heard back from you,
But I know how busy you are.
I check your web site
To follow your activities.
You'll be speaking tonight
About the ghosts in your book
At a local coffee house.
Please make time to write to me.
She knows
That I have contacted you.

II

Her whining was deafening
But it has quieted some.
She ventures out more often,
Hovering
Around my room,
Avoiding contact,
Clinging desperately to the walls
Like a blown up balloon
Rubbed against a kid's hair
Charged with static electricity.

III

She came at first
As a face without an expression,
Floating
Above me,
And I awoke in my bed
Sweating and startled
But not afraid of her.
I knew somehow
She wasn't there
To harm me.

IV

She has now learned
How to enter my dreams.
I see her
As she must have looked
Before her death,
Pretty,
With long blonde hair
Hanging to her shoulders
And blue
Piercing eyes.

V

I see her
In my sleep,
Running alone,
Laughing.
It is a wonderful sound
That echoes
As if in a tunnel.
A pink ribbon is in her hair
And it bounces
As she runs.

VI

She stops at a swing set
In the woods
And mounts the swing
With her hands on the chains
High above her head,
Perfectly still, and still perfectly expressionless.
Not swinging,
Until a man
Comes up to her
And makes her smile.

VII

He is a shadow
At first,
As if the dream
Is taunting me.
Then he becomes clearer.
He walks behind her
And begins to push
Higher and higher.
Her laughter with his
Is music.

VIII

It is not *my* father
But I am glad for her.
His face and hers
Are filled with happiness
As the swing swings higher,
Until he stops it
From moving.
She runs from it and him
Across the lawn
Running faster and faster.

IX

I watch him
Alone at the swing
Staring after her,
Sad.
His short dark hair
Thinning
Parted on the left,
His beard a shadow
On a handsome
Face.

X

Then she is alone again
Standing by a wooden bridge,
Her hands on her face.
She is crying,
No,
Whimpering
I recognize those sounds.
I sit up in my bed
And listen
As they come through my closet door.

CHAPTER II

Voices

Part 1

I

Her name is Melinda.

I don't know how

I know this

But it came to me

In another dream.

Someone was calling her.

Melinda.

She was standing over me

Staring

Her eyes looking into mine.

II

She was

Expressionless again.

Nothing betrayed her thoughts

Then

Slowly

Her lips began to move

Upward.

Her smile,

Beautiful and haunting,

Woke me

III

I sat up
With an urgency
To call your number.
I found it on your web site
And memorized it for times like this,
But the clock
Said midnight.
I knew I couldn't call.
I wished that you would finally answer
My emails.

IV

I trust you to know
What I am experiencing.
My mother's concerned.
I will never get her to believe
That spirits like Melinda live here.
They call on people
Like us
For help.
It is perfectly natural
For those of us willing to believe.

V

Do you hear her
A voice
That calls out from somewhere?
Soft moans
Or whining
That reach deep inside of you
Begging,
Pleading for you to understand,
A soft whisper
That says Melinda?

VI

Or maybe
Melinda isn't the one calling to you.
Maybe
You hear
A male voice,
A father who is calling out
To his son.
A desperate plea
For you
To talk to me.

VII

Billy Joel sang
"Only the Good Die Young."
I play it often in my room.
Have you spoken
To many dead people
Who have died young?
Are they still here
To talk about their lives?
Will they be okay?
Was my father killed because he was good?

VIII

When you were young
Did your parents say
Finish everything
On your plate
Or you will
Stay there
Until you do?
Does God keep us here
Until we finish
Everything we have started?

IX

Do you dream
At night?
Do you wake in a cold sweat
Knowing that what you have just heard
Is what you were meant to hear?
Do they struggle
To end your pain
Through them
Or end their pain
Through you?

X

How old were you
When you first began
To hear the voices
Of the dead?
Did you keep it secret?
Did anyone laugh
Or tease you
Or stop calling
And start
Saying prayers for you?

Part 2

I

The voices began
When I was fourteen.
My father is the only one
Who knew I heard them.
He told me
Not to be afraid.
He said they were
Like lost and lonely angels
And that His voices
Began at fourteen too.

II

Does everyone hear voices?
I asked my father.
No, he said
You and I were chosen as sort of Earth Angels.
We are special.
Do you only see them in your dreams?
Yes, I said
Do they scare you?
No, I answered.
Good, you needn't be afraid

III

Can Mom hear them?

I asked.

Your mom is the best mother

In the world,

He said.

But she doesn't understand

So she's afraid

Of what we hear and dream.

What do you say

We make your gift our secret.

IV

Who are they? I asked.

People with a message, he said.

Some have come for your help.

Do you want to help them? he asked.

Yes, I said.

Good, he answered,

Me too.

Come to me

If you have any questions.

I will be here for you.

V

My father is no longer
Alive as he was in this world.
And I know he is not dead.
His food is still on his plate.
He is not finished with his life here
Or me.
Why won't he answer?
Where has he been for eighteen months?
Why is he not
Communicating?

VI

The girl in my closet,
Melinda,
Did not come here
Until one year from my father's death.
Did he send her?
Is he talking through her?
Can he talk through you?
Why is it taking him so long to reach me?
Can you interpret dreams
From the Other Side?

VII

My father said
There are many people
Who say they hear voices.
They write books
And movies
And give lectures
But are not truly connected.
Why am I not
Connecting
To you?

VIII

Do spirits
Have frequencies?
Are they like radio waves
That seek transmitters?
How do the undead
Reconnect with the living?
How do they
Choose their listeners
And reach
Those of us who want to listen?

IX

My dreams
Have been taken over
By Melinda.
There are no nights now
When she doesn't come to me.
She comes out of her closet
A mass of energy
Floating
Until I am pushed
Into my dreams.

X

Some dreams
Are too real
Then
They make no sense.
They change so quickly.
In them I see Melinda.
The man at the swings
Comes back in shadows.
Is the sad man my father
And the crying Melinda me?

Part 3

I

The police
Said my mother
Had to go to the morgue
To identify the body.
I made her take me
To see if I could reach him.
He was on a table
With a sheet over his face.
When they lifted it
We saw him.

II

He did not appear
To be asleep.
His eyes
Were closed
And his face
Badly bruised,
No frown or anger
Or smile
An expressionless face
Like Melinda's

III

I tried to make him hear me,
Quietly
From inside my head,
And waited for his answer.
But it didn't come.
I screamed silently
Are you okay?
But there still was no answer.
I stood there waiting
Until I was led away crying.

IV

My mother made them tell her
What had happened.
A family,
Children and parents
In costumes,
Hit him head on
And killed him instantly.
He was pronounced dead
At the scene,
The only fatality.

V

They told us
Where the car had been taken
And gave us two boxes.
One had all of his personal belongings,
His clothes and wallet and jewelry.
The other
Was smaller than a breadbox
Wrapped in colorful paper
With a bow and card
That said Happy Birthday Son.

VI

The present
Is still in my closet
With Melinda;
It is in one corner
She
Is in the other.
I refuse to open it
Until
He says
I can.

VII

I don't know
What religion you are.
We are Catholics.
When people we love
Die
We take them to be embalmed
And put them
In their caskets
With the lid open
For people to see.

VIII

Friends and relatives came for two days
To see my father's body
Surrounded with beautiful flowers
From everyone.
They stood in line
To get the chance
To kneel and see his face close up
One last time
Before never
Seeing him again.

IX

The room was filled with chairs.
I sat in the front row
With my mother
To hug and kiss
And shake hands
With All of the guests
Who came to pay their respects.
Between the hugs
I sat and stared at him,
Waiting.

X

On the morning of his burial
I didn't want to go to his grave site.
I had never been
To a cemetery.
My father didn't like going there.
He told me I wasn't ready for it either.
When his hearse pulled in
Our limousine followed
And I knew
Why I should have listened.

CHAPTER III

MY FATHER

AND

FRIENDS

Part 1

I

Their voices began in chaos at the gate,

All of them talking at once,

A cacophony of frantic questions

From everywhere,

Hundreds of voices penetrating my skull.

I pressed my hands against my ears

Trying to block them out

But the voices came

From somewhere deep

Inside my head.

II

I couldn't bear to hear them

And screamed for them to

Stop!

The driver did.

I ran from the car

Back to the gate

With my mother shouting behind me.

She let me run.

I stood outside the cemetery gasping for air

Until the voices were finally silent.

III

The procession of cars
Passed with their headlights on and continued
To the side of the little road by the grave site.
They all thought they understood
And left me to be alone.
I watched from a distance
As they crawled from their cars
And surrounded the flowers piled near his coffin,
Hundreds of flowers
That died for him.

IV

The people stood in a circle
Staring into the center
Where the coffin sat above his grave,
Then another car passed me
And parked by them to unload its passengers,
A family of four
From a newspaper clipping
In their funeral clothes
Instead of their
Halloween costumes

V

I don't know
If my mother
Let them stay.
I turned and walked
For miles
Angry and cursing
At my father
For leaving me,
Saying things
He would have never tolerated.

VI

Do you go to cemeteries?
Can you hear them?
Do they
Call out to you
To help them?
Are they in pain?
Will they ever be free?
Why don't I see
Or hear from him?
Why can't he talk to me?

VII

The light was on when I returned home.
My mother was sleeping in a chair.
I went to my room and stood for a long time
Staring at my closet door
Waiting for him to speak to me.
My father's present was sitting in there
Where my mother had placed it.
There were no sounds from the closet
Until my birthday
One year later.

VIII

When I reached for the box
I felt her energy
Sliding first across
The back of my hand
Then up my arm
Into my neck and shoulders.
A chill ran through me,
Ice
Then fire
Then comfort

IX

I have never tried
To touch the box since.
Can the things
People touch
Before they die
Carry a piece
Of their souls?
Can they carry messages
We are meant
To understand?

X

What will our spirits
Look like
When we return?
Will we look the way we did
At the time of our death?
Will we resemble who we were,
Or be floating masses of shapeless energy
Only visible on this side
In dreams and visions
That must be interpreted?

Part 2

I

In a couple of months
I will graduate
From high school.
I have already made plans
For community college.
My father would not have been happy
But we can't afford a four year school
And my mother needs me here
To take care of the house
And her.

II

I haven't said much to you
About my friends.
There isn't much to say.
I've had very little
Contact with them since my father's passing.
They are computer geeks
And treat their
Computers
As if they are
Girlfriends.

III

Most of their time
Is spent goggling
Over their electronic lovers
They keep snuggled
Near their beds.
They hurry to get home
So they can excitedly run their fingers
Across them
With little time or thought
For anything else.

IV

My mother surprised me
This year
With a birthday party
And invited all three of them.
Surprise I said,
And ignored them
While I sat playing games
And writing diary poems
On my laptop
Until they left.

V

George, Todd, Eric

And I

Have been friends since kindergarten.

There is very little

We don't know about each other

But I never told them

About my "gift"

Until my father died.

They listened

Then laughed.

VI

You realize

Todd said

That this is part of

Your grieving process.

You need to believe that he is still here.

You need to embrace it

Until you can get over it,

Then let him go.

You still have us he said,

And laughed.

VII

Todd is right

George said.

We all loved your father.

He was great

But nobody lives forever.

You have to think about

Where to go from here.

Think about college

And your career

Not ghosts.

VIII

With your grades and IQ

You can be anything you want.

Focus on that Eric said.

Do it for your father.

We all know what we want to be

And where we want to go.

Pick a school

And career.

You can't make money

Being a ghost buster.

IX

Growing up
Can be scary.
One day can change
Everything and everyone
You ever knew.
I stopped hanging with them.
They laughed at first
Saying I should get over it
Then tried to talk more seriously
When it was too late.

X

I spend time
Writing poems in my room
Trying to make sense
Of life and death
The way millions of others have done before me,
Brilliant people of all religions and some with none,
Great minds,
Isn't it amazing that not one of them
Has returned to us
With a definitive answer about the After Life.

Part 3

I

I have never had a girlfriend
And I am not gay.
George sort of has a girlfriend
That he met on line.
Todd is his own girlfriend.
Eric is
Openly gay.
They will all most likely meet someone
Away at college
While I am here getting to know me.

II

My mother
Is a widow.
She doesn't wear black every day
Like old women in mourning
But her mind and heart
Are dressed in black.
She has no desire
To marry again
But desperately wants a partner,
For me.

III

I am sure
You have a daughter
Or a cousin's friend
Who needs a boyfriend
Exactly like me.
My mother thinks everyone does.
She says prayers for good partners
Every day of the week
But I have enough on my mind
With Melinda.

IV

The Junior Prom
Was a couple of months
After my father died.
George and Todd
Both went with girls
Their mothers got for them.
Eric brought
A boyfriend
And made
All the local papers.

V

The Senior Ball
Is coming.
George is taking
The girl he took last year,
Todd has a steady girlfriend,
Eric is still not sure who he's taking.
I'm going with
My mother's friend's cousin
Because I'm tired of
Saying no.

VI

My mother is driving us
In the car she bought
With the insurance money
She received
From my father's accident.
We still have not fully settled
His claim.
My mother said when we do
She will quit work
And I will go to a good college.

VII

It has been two months
Since I started
Writing to you.
I imagine
That you're not even getting these.
Why else would you
Not be answering?
And though my father
Hasn't answered me either
I won't stop trying to reach either of you.

VIII

If people stopped praying
Every time they didn't get answered
There would be no prayers.
I know my father
Is trying to reach me.
I feel his presence
And know the key
Is Melinda.
She is still in my closet
Opposite the corner from his present to me.

IX

She has become
More daring.
She moans and whines less
And appears to me more often
Still hovering
Watching
Floating
Rubbing up against me
Wearing my body
Like an old suit.

X

The dreams
Haven't stopped.
She comes to me in them
Every night
With her pink ribbon bouncing
And the handsome man
In the shadows
Constantly around her
Watching her
And me.

CHAPTER IV

THE ACCIDENT

Part 1

I

I wasn't able to handle

The details of the crash

Or the family that caused it until recently

Even though I had seen them at the cemetery.

I feared my reaction.

The parents are younger than mine.

The son

Is about twelve

And the daughter

Is about nine.

II

I went to the library

And looked up what had happened

In our local paper.

There was a picture of my father

Young and smiling

I wanted to burst into tears.

I put the paper down

And took a walk,

When I got back

The paper was still there waiting for me.

III

It was a dark and stormy night.
In some places
Halloween was canceled.
Wind tore through neighborhoods
Blowing down trees and power lines.
Rain pelted brave trick-or-treaters
Forcing them to re-treat.
The only ones
Foolish enough to be driving
Were rushing home to their families.

IV

The McCannisters were returning
From a canceled party.
The rain had graduated
To a downpour.
They were less than a mile
From home
On the highway doing 40
When the children began to argue
Their father turned to quiet them
Entering my father's lane.

V

Have you ever seen
Flowers by the roadside?
Shrines to those who died there?
Can souls get trapped
In the spot where they were killed?
Can they be forced to linger
And relive their death
Again and again?
If it is true and my father was there
He wasn't answering.

VI

When I left the spot
Where he died
I walked toward their house.
I had no idea what I would say
If I saw any of them.
When I turned the corner
And stood
By their mail box
It was overstuffed.
A For Sale sign was on the lawn.

VII

Do people
Take their guilt with them
When they die?
Are they forced to relive
Their mistakes
Until they are free from them?
Do they live in limbo forever?
How long does it take
To Cross Over?
Can good people go directly to the Light?

VIII

What is death?
What does it look like?
I asked my father.
I don't know he said.
I know it has to do with the Light.
A very bright light.
Have you seen it? I asked
I have he said.
I've watched troubled souls
Walk off into it.

IX

Did you help set them free?
Yes he said. I believe I did.
Am I able to help them too?
Is that my gift?
I believe it is he said.
If you want it to be.
Would I be able to help you
If you got trapped?
I hope so he said
And smiled.

X

Can people
Who save
Tortured souls
Go directly
To the Light
Without stopping?
If they do
Will they lose
Their power
To communicate with the living?

Part 2

I

I hope you do not find
My diary poems
Annoying.
My mother has trouble reading them.
She said they are like
Machine gun fire
Shooting ideas at her.
I stopped letting her read them
When I was about
Fourteen.

II

My father of course
Loved them.
He asked me to teach him
How I do it.
I just write them I said
As I think of things.
It helps me
To focus
And becomes sort of
Poet-therapy.

III

Do you have someone
Or something
To help you
When you need
To talk?
Do you have a wife
Or son or daughter
To share
Your secrets
And your spirits?

IV

My father
Tried to write
Diary poems
But they were not very good
Except the ones
He wrote
About my mother
And me.
I told him he should write about the voices.
No, he said.

V

Are you afraid of

Your gift?

Do you ask yourself

Why me?

Do you spend

Most of your time alive

Thinking about dying?

Do you wonder

When all of the questions will stop

And all of the answers will begin to come?

VI

Melinda's dreams

Are sometimes so frightening

I wake up

Unable to breathe.

I'm in them

Being warned.

I'm trying to understand her

But I can't.

I scream at her to make sense

But she doesn't.

VII

The man in the shadows
Is in the dreams too.
He laughs
At first
When Melinda
Talks to me and
I don't understand her.
Then he stops laughing
And begins whining.
I wake up to the noises in my closet.

VIII

I dreamed of her one night
When the man wasn't there.
It was as if
She was someone else.
We were alone
And her blue eyes paralyzed me,
Pulled me inside out,
And when she said LET GO and I did
I began falling
At an incredible speed.

IX

I was falling faster
And faster
With each second,
The fear building inside of me.
Frantically I searched for something to grab
Something to break my fall.
There were hands
Attached to corpses
Hundreds of naked bodies
From photos I had seen.

X

I wanted to turn from them
But I needed them
To catch me
To stop me from falling.
I screamed for them
To please help me
But my mother came instead
And asked me if I was having
A bad dream.
Yes, I said.

Part3

I

Where do bodies go?

Do they unite with the soul

Years and years later

After they are done rotting?

Or do they simply become

Recycled dust?

Old rubbish?

Discarded Cicada shells?

Or maybe

Abandoned caterpillar cocoons?

II

Do souls like Melinda

Get lonely

For the living?

Do they spend eternity

Pining for what they've lost?

Would the dead

Call to the living

Pleading for them to come

To end their loneliness

And cut short their own lives here?

III

I am not

Contemplating suicide.

I don't think my father

Would want me to go to them early.

We both know I can only help them from here.

But I don't really know Melinda.

What if Melinda

Is not

From my father

At all?

IV

Has Melinda

Lost a father?

Does she need someone

To talk to

The way that I need you?

Would she take me

Into her power

Through my dreams

And convince me to

Join her?

V

My mother's friend's cousin's daughter
Wants to meet me.
My mother said she will be
The perfect date.
She has a great personality
Which in mother-talk
Usually means
She is probably
The ugliest girl
In her graduating class.

VI

I wanted to tell her
That I had changed my mind.
I didn't want to go
To the stupid Senior Ball.
She said I should
Get out of the house.
I would really like her.
She is fun to be with,
Has long pretty hair
And piercing eyes.

VII

Can souls change bodies?
Is reincarnation real?
Is life here on earth
The beginning
Or end
Of a cycle of lives?
Is my father living again
In some other form?
Is there any way
To recognize him?

VIII

My father and I
Saw a girl once
Who was not like
Other young girls.
She said things
And knew things
My father couldn't understand.
He called her
An old soul.
Can old souls live in new bodies?

IX

Can you see old souls

In new bodies? I asked my father.

I'm not sure, he said.

But sometimes I think I can.

Sometimes people seem so familiar

I swear I know them

Even when

I know

I have never

Seen them before.

X

When dogs

Go around

Smelling each others butts

Do you think

They are trying to find

Their old souls?

I asked my father.

He nearly fell off his chair laughing

Then said,

I'm not really sure.

CHAPTER V

KATIE

Part I

I

When the doorbell rang
My heart nearly stopped.
I knew who was on the doorstep.
My mother had invited
Her friend's cousin's daughter
Katie
To dinner
So we could
Get to know each other
Before our first date.

II

I felt the sweat beading up
In my arm pits
And my hand
Was actually shaking.
When I opened the door
There they were
Mother and daughter,
Neither of them
Even coming close
To looking like Melinda.

III

I guess I was staring
Because my mother said,
Where are your manners?
Invite them in.
Katie wasn't anything I imagined.
I wanted to take a picture of her
And send it to the geeks.
They would have crapped their pants
And said I rented her for the photo.
Then reality hit.

IV

Did you ever realize
That you were too awake?
Did you wish you really were dreaming
Because what you had was too good to be real?
Why would someone like Katie
Ever want someone
Like me?
And then I glimpsed her
In the mirror behind me.
She was shaking her head yes at her mother.

V

Melinda has long blonde hair

And piercing blue eyes.

Katie

Is a brunette

With warm hazel eyes

That are almost green.

Her nose turns up

And her freckles

Look like they were placed there.

Do you believe in love at first sight?

VI

I couldn't take my eyes off of her.

My mother

Gave me the

Don't-Do-That look,

But I did it anyway

And I think Katie

Liked it

Because she was staring back at me.

Both her eyes and her freckles

Looked like they were dancing.

VII

After dinner
Our mothers let us
Take a walk together.
I can't believe I
Took her hand as we walked
And she let me.
I didn't think you would be
So good looking, she said.
I was so surprised
I squeezed and almost broke her hand.

VIII

I told her
I was sorry.
Then I said
Squeeze mine.
She said
What?
I said I want to be sure I'm not dreaming.
She smiled an amazing smile
And I said
Will you come to the dance with me?

IX

When we got back into the house
My mother asked if we enjoyed our walk.
It was okay, I said.
Katie looked shocked
So I burst out laughing.
She smacked me.
She actually smacked me.
We both cracked up laughing.
When she left to go home
I wished she didn't

X

I told my mother I really liked Katie
And hurried to my room
Because I knew
Something was not right.
It was too perfect
Too unreal.
No noise was coming from the closet
So I sat on my bed and waited
For this dream
To suddenly end.

Part 2

I

I sat for nearly
One hour
Thinking about Katie
Melinda
And my father.
Did he send her?
Is it possible
For the dead to manipulate life?
Has he become
My guardian angel?

II

I jumped
When I heard the knock at my door.
It was my mother
Smiling
Telling me that the phone
Was for me.
I don't have a cell phone because I don't like phones,
But we talked
For four hours
Then switched to emails.

III

We talked about everything,
School, neighbors, friendships
And fathers.
I told her about mine.
She told me about her parents'
Divorce.
Her father lives far away.
She hasn't seen him in over a year.
And is an only child
Like me

IV

Did you ever say something
You wish you didn't say?
Did you share a secret
You were not supposed to share
And then wait to see if
Something would happen?
I wanted to tell her that I have been writing
Diary poems to you
About my father who had a special gift,
But I couldn't tell her

V

Katie said

Her father's only gift to her

Was leaving.

All her parents did was fight

And hate each other.

He still loves Katie

But he is not able to communicate with her

Just yet.

It hurts but she sort of understands.

Can I teach her how to write diary poems?

VI

Katie lives a few miles from us.

It's way too far to walk.

She doesn't go to my school

But no place is too far

For telephones or computers.

When I finally got to bed

That first night I met her

It wasn't until three in the morning.

The minute I fell asleep

I started dreaming

VII

Melinda

Was at the wooden bridge

Crying

And the man from the shadows

Was standing over her.

The man reached out his hand

And Melinda pulled away.

The man reached for her again.

She tried to run

But the railing gave way.

VIII

I heard myself

Screaming.

I wanted to reach for her

To save her.

I could see her falling down

Faster and faster.

The corpses' hands were reaching out

To catch her but they couldn't

And my mother's voice

Asked me if I was having another bad dream.

IX

I was still awake
When the sun came up.
Melinda's whimpering
Would not let me sleep.
She had entered me somehow.
I could feel her
Wearing me,
Writhing under my skin
Trying to find a place
To be safe.

X

It was Saturday.
There was no reason to get out of bed,
Except to check my email.
Somehow
I fell into a dreamless sleep.
I awoke with a start
And ran to the computer.
I was hoping there would be an email
From Katie.
There were thirty-six

Part 3

I

They started with

I just wanted to say good morning

And ended with something like

If you are not alive

I will never forgive you.

I sat there staring at the screen

Not believing

She was real.

Then I touched the screen

To help myself see her again.

II

I wrote her a diary poem that said

You will be happy to know

(I hope)

That I am still alive

And would love to see you again.

If it's okay with you and your mother

We can go for pizza or something later today

To talk about the dance.

If you can't or it's too soon to see me again

Maybe we can go another time.

III

My mother was thrilled
When I told her about the pizza date.
She said she would drive me
And Katie's mother could drive her.
We could all have pizza together.
Oh yeah what a great idea,
I said.
No!
Don't even
Think about it.

IV

It took about an hour
To figure out
What to wear.
I finally settled on a red flannel shirt
And jeans
Then I combed my hair
About twelve times
Before I left for the car.
I touched my closet door
But didn't hear or feel a thing.

V

We got to the pizzeria first

And got a booth.

My mother sat with me.

When Katie came in with her mother

We all stood and stared for a minute.

Katie was wearing a red flannel shirt

And jeans, like me

We all laughed hard,

Then at almost the exact same time,

We said *okay, good-bye* to our mothers.

VI

The waitress came over

And I asked if I should order a whole pizza.

Yes, she said, with pepperoni.

Do you like pepperoni?

I do, I said.

Good she answered

I'm starving.

We didn't say much for a while

And just when she was about to ask me something

They must have come in.

VII

Katie
Doesn't look like other girls I know.
She doesn't wear make-up
Or have a fancy hair-do.
She's sort of a country-girl.
I was so busy admiring her
I didn't see them until they were in front of us.
Check this out Eric said.
The look on all three of their faces
Was priceless.

VIII

They would have stared all day
With their mouths wide open and speechless.
It felt so good I almost let them,
But I said
This is Katie.
Katie this is George, Todd and Eric.
Holy Sh*t Todd whispered.
It's amazing to meet you George said.
Okay
You can all go now I told them

IX

Todd, Eric and George
Sat in a booth on the far side gawking
While I sat eating and talking
With Katie.
She wanted to know all about them.
I told her how long we had been friends.
She asked if they were going to the dance.
I said I didn't know because we weren't really
Talking right now
But didn't tell her why

X

We ate the whole pizza
Then we discussed
The dance.
I can't believe it's next week
She said.
Are you sure you want to take me?
You can change your mind if you want.
I looked up at her and smiled
Then I saw something strange
In the center of her hazel eyes.

CHAPTER VI

THE

CEMETERY

Part 1

I

That night

Melinda spoke to me.

She hovered over my bed

And when I

Opened my eyes

Hers were staring

Into mine.

You mustn't fear the voices,

She said.

Go to the cemetery.

II

I awoke as I usually do

From dreams like that

Cold and sweaty.

My room was totally silent.

I looked at my closet and stared

Through the darkness

Then got up from my bed.

When I went to open my closet door

It opened

By itself.

III

I could barely breathe.
I thought for sure my mother
Would be knocking at the door.
My heartbeat seemed almost deafening.
Slowly I fell to my knees.
As I reached for my father's present
Melinda did as she had done before,
She entered me through my hand
And climbed through me slowly
Until every part of me was filled with her.

IV

I stayed on my knees for what seemed to be hours
Frozen to the spot.
A dream passed through me
As if each of the thoughts in the dream were mine.
Melinda was with the man
From the shadows.
His face was clear.
He was holding Melinda's hand.
They were standing by a grave stone
Looking out toward the gate.

V

They turned to each other
And the same dream I had before
Began to play again.
Melinda
Was at the wooden bridge
Crying.
The man from the shadows
Was standing over her shouting.
When the man reached out his hand to grab her,Aa
Melinda pulled taking both of them over the edge.

VI

I heard myself
Screaming.
I wanted to reach for them
To save them.
I could see them falling
Faster and faster.
The corpses' hands were reaching out
To catch them but they couldn't
And my mother's voice
Asked me if I was having another bad dream.

VII

Her hand touched my shoulders from behind me.
I jumped when I felt her.
I thought she was Melinda.
She helped me to my feet
And led me to my bed
Then sat beside me.
Do you hear the voices?
She asked.
Is someone in your closet?
Has your father come back?

VIII

No
I said.
I haven't heard from him yet.
I thought you might hear the voices
The way he did,
She said.
You knew about his voices?
I asked.
Yes, she said.
But I never let him talk about them.

IX

Were you afraid of them? I asked
Terrified, she said
I thought if he
Told me about them
They would start visiting me
And I knew I couldn't handle it.
Are you still afraid? I asked.
I am still terrified,
But I want you to tell me
Everything.

X

We sat until the sun came out.
I didn't miss a detail.
I read her every email
I've written to you.
When I was done
She said I should sleep for awhile
Then
We should go
Together
To the cemetery.

Part 2

I

My mother was sitting at the table.
She was fully dressed and ready.
So was I.
We got into the car without talking
And drove straight to the cemetery gate.
As we approached
I felt myself shaking.
I wanted to run from the car
But Melinda was there inside of me
Forcing me to continue on.

II

I held my breath
And listened for the deluge,
But nothing came.
My mother looked at me
As if to say are you okay?
I don't hear them, I said.
I think Melinda asked them not to speak.
She doesn't want me to be afraid and is with me.
I'm sure, my mother said,
That your father is with us too.

III

She pulled bravely to the side of the little road
And turned off the engine.
We went to his stone.
I expected to hear his voice then
And begged him to say something.
There was silence.
My body moved without me.
I walked as my mother followed
To a stone near my father's grave.
My mother gasped.

IV

The stone read
Rest In Peace
Melinda Johnson Age 9.
My skin began to tingle.
Burn.
I wanted to run
But my feet were anchored to her grave site.
When my feet were free to move again
They went to the stone
Next to Melinda's.

V

I could see his sad face in my mind
As clearly as it had appeared
In my dream
And then I heard the weeping.
My mother was crying.
I know this story
She said.
It happened over 20 years ago
Right after we moved in.
It was heart breaking.

VI

The whining was deafening
It came from inside of me,
Then became a whimper
As my mother told the story
That made the headlines
Of the man who killed his daughter
And himself
Rather than lose
His family
To divorce.

III

She's still alive
I screamed.
My mother stared at me in disbelief.
Melinda? she asked.
It can't be.
Her mother, I said.
She's still alive. Melinda is communicating with me.
My mother put her hands to her mouth.
Through her tears she said
I know where she lives.

VIII

I bent before my father's grave
And kissed it
Before going to the car
As the engine started
I heard a slow murmur.
It began to rise and get louder.
They were starting to talk!
All of them at once.
I begged my mother
To hurry out of the cemetery gates.

IX

The house was less than two blocks
From ours
Unkempt and sorrowful.
My insides were ready to explode
I wanted desperately to leave there
But I knew I couldn't.
I had to take her in there to tell her mother the truth
About Melinda and the accident.
My mother rang the bell and an old woman
Stood before us.

X

Are you Mrs. Johnson?
My mother asked.
The whining inside of me
Became a painful whimpering.
No, the woman said.
My mother and I stood there
Confused and speechless.
What do you want of her?
The woman asked.
She is not well.

Part 3

I

My mother lied
And said we were old friends
Making a Sunday visit.
The woman was skeptical
But allowed us into the bedroom
Where Melinda's mother lay dying.
I began to cry as I saw her frail body.
Are you death? she asked.
I thought you'd be bigger
She said, and attempted a smile

II

My son has a special gift, my mother told her.
You needn't tell me why you've come, she answered
I have always known it was an accident.
I knew she would find a way to bring me peace.
Bring her to me.
I walked closer to the bed and it was as if Melinda
Began electrocuting me.
The woman took my hand in hers
And Melinda flowed through me with a force that
Drained me of my strength.

III

My mother was terrified and sobbed loudly
As the woman's eyes closed.
She was smiling motionless and peaceful
Then
Her eyes jerked open.
Her voice was weak and barely audible.
We have something for you she whispered.
She pointed to her night stand
And there exactly as I had remembered it
Was the pink ribbon Melinda had worn in my dream.

IV

I let go of the woman's hand
And took the ribbon.
May you both
Have peace, I said.
She took my hand in both of hers.
May your own entry
Into the Light, she said,
Be as peaceful
As you have made
The possibility of ours

V

We were dismissed.
The other woman walked us to the door.
My sister knew you would come some day
She said.
She waited patiently and painfully.
God bless you
For bringing
My niece home to us.
Your reward
Will be in a better world

VI

When we got into the car
I felt strange
Empty
But happy.
I turned to say something to my mother
Who was crying.
I should have been more understanding
She said.
I should have shared these moments
With your father.

VII

When we got into the house
I went directly to my room
And opened the closet door.
Melinda
Was not there of course.
I reached into my pocket
Took out the pink ribbon
And placed it in her corner,
But before I shut the door
I checked for the box with my father's present to me.

VIII

At the computer
There were sixty-three emails from Katie,
Four from George, twelve from Eric
And none from Todd.
I opened Katie's first
And didn't know where to begin.
I invited her to come over
And two minutes after I pressed "send"
The phone rang.
You'd better have a good excuse she said

I went downstairs
To thank my mother
For coming with me.
She was sitting in
My father's chair
With his picture in her lap.
I miss him so much
She said.
I would give anything to see
Those hazel eyes alive again.

X

Katie
Is coming over
I said.
I want to open
Dad's present
And can't do it alone.
I want
To open it
With the three
Of you.

CHAPTER VII

Coincidences

Part 1

I

Katie came with her mother.

My mother asked

If we should go to my room.

Not yet, I said.

Is there something wrong?

Katie asked.

No

I said

I have something

To tell you.

II

We sat on my bed

And I started at the beginning

The way I did with my mother.

Before I knew it

She was sitting there wide-eyed

Crying.

I love what you can do

She said

And I love what you did

for Melinda.

III

Are you frightened by my ability to talk with them?
Not even a little
She said.
I think it's wonderful
That you can speak to them.
I want to read all of your diary poems.
Some of them are about you, I said.
They'd better be good things she answered.
There is nothing bad about you
I told her.

IV

She leaned into me.
I kissed her on the lips.
The tingling started somewhere inside me.
I almost thought Melinda had returned
But recognized it as my own heat rising.
We kissed again
And my mother interrupted us.
Is it time?
She asked.
For what? Katie asked.

V

I told her
My father brought a gift
For me the day he died.
When I spoke with him the day before
He said it was something special.
Is it smaller than a breadbox? I asked.
Yes, he said, but much more meaningful.
I told her I hadn't opened it yet.
Would she like to open it with me?
Oh my God yes she said

VI

Katie's mother was still in the room.
I let her stay.
I knew my father wouldn't mind.
I didn't want to be alone when I opened it.
All of their eyes were on me
As I brought the gift to the bed
My hands were shaking.
It was heavier than I remembered.
I removed the card and untaped the paper slowly,
Way too slowly for Katie and our mothers.

VII

They were hand-written books.
I opened the envelope and read the card
Dear Son
If you are reading this
I am already gone.
I would have taken this off the box
If I was wrong about my premonition.
I am afraid of what may happen today
But can do nothing
To stop it.

VIII

I suspect that my dream
Has become a reality.
Your mother and your new friends surround you
But I don't know how much time has passed.
I wish I could have been there
But I have been called
To where I was destined to be.
I suspect that all I anticipated
About Melinda has already happened.
Well done if it has.

IX

It is my hope
That she is the first
Of many souls
You will save.
You will not do it alone.
If you have not yet met her
You will, she is an Earth Angel too.
It is your fate to be with her.
Recognize her by the color of my eyes
And by the gift she will develop.

X

I looked up at Katie.
She was smiling.
It started when I was fourteen
She said.
I've kept it secret.
I stared at her in disbelief,
Then continued to read his letter.
Note that I have written this in diary poems.
Thank you for teaching me how to write them.
You will find more in the books I've written for you.

Part 2

I

His diary poems
Were the most amazing things
I have ever seen.
They are his thoughts
And experiences of
All the souls he has encountered
Through his lifetime.
They are his questions
And his answers
About the After Life.

II

I know now
Why I couldn't reach him.
His many years of soul saving
Earned him his immediate
Right of passage
To the Light
Beyond the troubled souls and the ability to
Communicate,
A right that Katie and I
Hope to earn someday.

III

He said he would love
To take credit for Katie
But she was always meant
To be with me.
We are destined for greatness.
His poems would guide us
Into sharing and understanding the purpose of life
On earth and in limbo
A time for living and loving
For repenting and dying and eternal peace.

IV

There are no
Insignificant people
And no such thing
As coincidence
All that happened to me
And *will* happen to me
Is in the books
And has always been.
We must accept who we are
And who we must be.

V

The night we opened the gift
We received two phone calls:
Mrs. Johnson
Died peacefully
In her sleep.
There would be no wake or open casket
Or visiting hours.
She was content to have lived a full life
And grateful
To be reunited with her loved ones

VI

The second call was from Katie.
Am I upset that I am destined
To be with her?
Yes, I said
Just kidding.
Not funny, she said,
And guess what
She got a call from her father
Who is sending her a ticket to come visit him.
She's going for a week sometime after the dance

VII

I don't know if you will ever read these
But my writing them
Has brought focus
And importance to my life.
I said when I began
Writing to you
That I believed dead people live here.
I know now they do.
I said I was helpless without you
I'm not

VIII

Perhaps someday
Our paths will cross
And I can thank you
For what you have helped me to do.
In the meantime
I have a tux to rent
And a limo to share
With George
Eric
And Todd

IX

By the way
I had a dream
The night we opened my father's gift.
Melinda's father was at the bridge
Melinda came to him and smiled.
They turned together holding hands
Standing at their stone in the cemetery.
They were looking at the gate waiting for someone
And then her mother
Came to join them.

X

There was another person in the dream,
A man in the shadows.
I couldn't see his face
But when he turned
To walk into the woods
Melinda and her parents followed him.
A beautiful bright light appeared.
They walked into it and,
As they turned to face me,
I saw my father smiling behind them.

ABOUT THE AUTHOR

V.T. Dacquino was a teacher in Westchester County, New York for many years and enjoys writing for both children and adults.

Some of his other books are:

Emails to a Paranormal: The Diary Poems of Damien Darrk

Mary Loved Daisies: The Diary Poems of Jim E. Lhyte

Hauntings of the Hudson River Valley: An Investigative Journey

Sybil Ludington: The Call to Arms

Return of the Cicada

Kiss the Candy Days Good-bye

Kiss the Candy Days Hello

www.ingramcontent.com/pod-product-compliance
Lightning Source LLC
Chambersburg PA
CBHW021213250626
47155CB00008B/2792